THE OUTLIERS

A NOVEL

JACK CLEMONS

SECANT PUBLISHING
Salisbury, Maryland

For information about this title, contact the publisher:

Secant Publishing, LLC
P.O. Box 4059
Salisbury MD 21803

www.secantpublishing.com

ISBN: 978-1-944962-91-3 (hardcover)
ISBN: 978-1-944962-92-0 (ebook)
Library of Congress Control Number: 2021907489

Book cover design by ebooklaunch.com

Historical images courtesy of the Lewes Historical Society

DEDICATION

While writing is a solitary occupation, this book could not have come together without the patience, invaluable assistance and advice of my wife and partner, Denise, herself an accomplished author.

1

I met the marshal almost thirty years ago. It was on a Friday. I couldn't forget the date, it was May 3, 1901, exactly one week before my brother died. I was out on the pier that day taking stock of visitors, steering for the girls, when the marshal got off the boat.

The early May air carried a bracing chill. Towners covered the pier like ants on a carcass. Even a whiff of good weather brought people out. I remember the ferry coming in from Cape May had to stand out off the breakwater while a freighter wallowed under steam and sails to tack out against the tide. We got traffic like that in season.

When the ferry steamed in, I got busy watching the men coming off, trying to figure who were traveling alone or passing through—maybe here on business or looking to lose money at the hotels' tables. Miss Lil had showed me what to look for. They carried small bags or none at all and never had somebody there to meet them. As soon as they set foot on the pier, they'd start checking for the ladies like crabbers dropping a line. They were easy to spot once you knew what to look for.

I worked fast because there'd be more men coming in when the fishing fleet tied up. Menhaden crews were harder to work. The crews were bone tired and had families in town. You could steer some of them, but it took more talking. Their boats came in at the Iron Pier, and I had to get done at Queen Anne's and get over there so Tommy Dallard couldn't beat me out. Trawler men couldn't pay much, plus the girls didn't care for the way they smelled. But Miss Lil hated losing seamen to the hotel girls Tommy steered for.

Anyway, the old man, that is how I thought of him that day, must have come off with the rest. I guess he didn't look like the sort to steer because I hadn't noticed him. But he'd been watching me and must have figured I was a local because he took hold of my arm and turned me like a spindle. He had a strong grip for an old guy, and he made me jump coming up behind me like that. I twisted around and shook off his hand and gave him a look to show him he shouldn't fool around with me. I had to raise my eyes to do it. I was tall for my age, but he was an inch or so taller than me. I didn't show it, but my stomach twitched. Being stared at by a white man could go either way. We watched each other for a second while the passengers pushed past us, heading who knew where now, but not to Miss Lil's.

Other than being tall, he wasn't much to look at. He had on a dusty grey suit that didn't fit well. He was carrying a beat-up leather satchel he set down next to his foot. It was hard to say how old he was—maybe fifty or so. His face was tanned like he'd spent time in the sun, but his cheeks and jaw hadn't gone loose like the skin does on older folks. His face was round at the top and pointed at the chin, and a thick mustache dropped off the sides of it. He would have looked comical if it weren't for his eyes. They were blue—not like summer skies—but pale and washed out. And the look behind them was hard.

"I'm lookin' for a man," he said. His voice was ragged, like a rusted saw. The way he talked sounded different from the way locals did.

"Sorry mister?"

"I need to find a man." He put his hand on my shoulder again.

"Can't help you there," I said. "I like girls myself." I knew what he meant, but I was annoyed. I pulled away.

"A particular man," he said, not bothering with my insult. "Name's Ryan."

"Don't know any Ryan."

"About thirty or so. Short fella, sandy-colored hair. Wears a skinny mustache." That sounded familiar but I wasn't going to tell him that. "I'll pay you a dollar to point him out."

He wanted to find him pretty bad to pay that kind of money to an Indian. But I didn't need his dollar.

"Don't know him," I said again and turned away.

"Might hang out with those ladies you work for."

That stopped me. I turned around.

"What's that supposed to mean?"

"Don't smoke me, boy. You seen this man or not?"

"I told you I didn't."

"Maybe. Where's your girls' house at? I'll ask the madam."

I stared him down a bit before I answered. He just looked back at me, not frowning, not squinting like he thought I was lying, just looking. That wasn't the stare I generally got when I was sassing whites.

"I don't know what you're talking about, mister."

He took a couple of steps toward me, so I added, "Try one of the hotels. Girls sometimes hang out in there."

"Hotels?"

He looked to his left, toward the Iron Pier. Miss Lil's place was right next to it, but I wasn't about to direct him there. I pointed the other way.

"The Ocean House or the Breakwater. Down the beach just off the road into town."

"Town? You mean Lewes?" He made it sound like loose, the way the Jersey tourists said it. Nobody from Delaware ever got it wrong.

"Lewes," I said, pronouncing it loo-is. "There're carriages that'll take you in for a nickel. Or you can wait for the train."

He looked at me like he thought I was being smart-mouthed, which I was. The train did come out there a couple times a week, but it wasn't scheduled anytime soon.

"I'll walk."

He picked up his traveling bag, stepped around me and headed down the pier. He walked like he had a purpose, not going fast, just intent on getting where he was going. Two carriages for hire passed by him going into town, but he ignored them.

I looked around. I'd wasted too much time jawing with him. The pier had almost emptied and the fishing boats were already docking at the Iron Pier. No point in rushing over there now. It was almost a mile across beach sand. Tommy would be working them hard before I showed up. I had to let it go for the day.

2

I took a back way into town and then circled around to the street where Hannah lived. I was hoping she'd be out in the yard or on her porch, but she wasn't. She should have been home from school by then, so either she wasn't there or she was ignoring me. I thought about knocking on the door, but except for Miss Lil's, I'd never been inside a white person's house. So I just walked up and down the opposite side of the street a while, making a fool of myself and hoping her father wouldn't come home or a neighbor wouldn't come out and chase me off.

I got back to Miss Lil's well past suppertime. This was before the fire, so she was in that two-story house next to the Iron Pier. All the girls had eaten by then and were upstairs dolling up for the evening trade. A hotel across from Miss Lil's provided a regular supply of visiting men willing to pay. It was the only hotel on that end of the beach.

Margaret, the colored woman who cooked and kept house for us, stretched over the sink, putting dishes and silver away in the cabinets. She gave me a smile as I came in. Margaret was good at her work and Miss Lil paid her handsomely for it.

"My lands, Master Sonny. You must be starvin'. Sit down there 'til I get you somethin'."

The kitchen still smelled good from her cooking. I realized I was hungry and sat. Margaret ladled hot crab stew into a crock bowl and put it in front of me along with a spoon. Normally, she would have chit-chatted with me while I ate, but Miss Lil came into the kitchen just then.

"Where have you been?"

The look she gave me wasn't quite a frown, but it was enough to let me know she was disappointed I'd been so late. After I finished up at the pier, my time was my own until supper. But it was well past that.

"Yes, ma'am. I'm sorry. I lost track of time."

"I suppose you did."

She wore red lipstick and had painted blue lines over her eyes. Her lacy black dress had a scooped-out front that put her bosom in view. The sight of her stirred me a little, which discomfited me. She was the boss, but she was only a little older than the girls—and a very handsome lady. Black was the only color I ever saw her in.

"Didn't have much ferry trade come in," she said. "Must have been slim pickings even for a Tuesday?"

"No, ma'am. That wasn't it. I got distracted and didn't tend to my steering."

She insisted I never lie to her, and I hardly ever did.

"Distracted. By what, might I ask?"

"Some old guy on the pier. He came off the ferry and marched up and asked if I'd seen some man he was looking for."

"He must have been a determined one for you to miss a ferry full of passengers."

"Yes, ma'am. He was. Told him I couldn't help him, but he wouldn't let it be. He knew I was steering for girls too, even though I never said anything about it."

"Did he say who he was looking for?"

"He said it was a man named Ryan. Seemed to think he might be hanging around with a working lady. I steered him to the hotels on the other end of beach."

"He paid you?"

"No. I mean I pointed him down that way. I didn't want him to come sniffing around here."

"Ryan?" She looked like she might know the name, but then she shook her head like she did when she decided to think no more of it. "Well, try not to get distracted tonight. Tend to the sheets and chamber pots whenever the girls are downstairs, make sure they have clean water and towels, and watch the back door for the rowdies."

"Yes, ma'am."

She kept a shotgun behind the desk off the parlor to keep the loutish kind away. I cleaned and oiled it every night.

"And check the wood for the upstairs stove. It could get chilly tonight."

"Yes, ma'am."

"Oh, and keep an eye out for Officer Hickman. The mayor's sending him out this evening. He needs a report for town council again this month."

I nodded. The police mostly let us be, but whenever some towner swore out a complaint, the mayor had to pretend he'd served a warrant.

"If I don't see him, take his paper and give him my regards."

"Yes, ma'am."

"Margaret's baked a strawberry pie. Offer him a slice or two of that pie you baked, Margaret. Strawberry's his favorite."

"Yesum. I will."

"And after you get caught up, Sonny, relieve Cornell for his break."

Cornell was the colored piano player Miss Lil sometimes hired. The clients coming from next door must be big ones. Playing piano was one of the few useful things I'd learned at the Carlisle school. I wasn't very good at it, but the customers weren't there for the music.

"Yes, ma'am."

She smiled at me and I knew she'd gotten over my being late. The front knocker clattered and Miss Lil went out to see to it.

On the way back to Miss Lil's, I decided I'd ask Anne about

Hannah. Anne was one of the older girls. She'd asked me to do some things for her in town, and I owed her a talk anyway. But she was in her room prettying up, so that would have to wait until morning. Instead, I put my mind to my chores. I felt bad for not having done so earlier.

It was after nine when a hard rap rattled the back door. I remember the time because the policeman, Hickman, had shown up at eight and sat out in the kitchen for an hour and ate half the pie and drank lots of black coffee. I think he was hoping one of the girls would come in and he could take a gander. He never gave us any papers. It wasn't too long after he left that somebody knocked.

Margaret was a little frightened by the rapping, since we weren't expecting anybody else. Once Officer Hickman came and went, we wouldn't see him again until the next time. She asked me if we should get the gun. I shook my head and cracked the door to look out.

"It's okay, Margaret," I said. "It's Jimmy."

I opened the door. The man who'd knocked had stepped back into the yard and was looking around while he waited. Not sure what he was looking for as dark as it was. Jimmy could dress like a dandy when he wanted to, but that night he had on a cotton shirt with the collar open and a canvas jacket that had seen lots of rain.

"Hey there, kid. How are things this evening?"

He stepped up onto the porch and came on inside without asking.

"Anne's busy tonight, Jimmy," I said. "I don't think she'll welcome company."

He pulled off his coat, plopped it over the back of a chair and then swung that around to sit down like he was straddling a horse.

"Company? When did I get to be company?"

He grinned to show me he was joking. When he smiled, his face got as round as a full moon. He brushed some stray hair off his forehead, but it drooped again. He was pretty easy to like—at least sometimes.

"You know what I mean. She's with a man."

"A man? With my Anne? Why, I should go up there and thrash

them both." He looked up at Margaret, who was taking it all in. "You're looking good this evening, Margaret. Might I have a slice of the pie that policeman didn't finish, or are you too busy for my attentions too?" Guess he'd been lurking out back waiting for Officer Hickman to leave.

"Of course you can have some, Mr. Lowe," Margaret said. "You know you're welcome here."

She sliced off a big piece and scooped it onto a stoneware plate and then poured him some coffee in a mug.

"It could be quite a while," I said, meaning Anne.

He turned the chair around again and sat down facing the table. He put a forkful into his mouth slowly like he didn't want to rush the occasion.

"It's wonderful, Margaret. This may be one of your best."

He closed his eyes while he chewed like he'd never had better.

"That's fine," he said to me then. "I'm not going anywhere."

I was standing next to the table and he reached up to ruffle my hair. I pulled away.

"Didn't they teach you any patience up at that Indian school, kid? Or were you asleep during class?"

Though he teased me a lot, he never acted like he had anything against Indians. I pushed my hair back over my ears.

"I don't have time for patience now, Jimmy."

He didn't like that name very much. He'd told us his name was Jim Lowe, but Anne had called him Jimmy when she introduced him and because she used it on him, he couldn't get too cross if I did. And because he insisted on calling me kid all the time, I decided I would call him Jimmy. Anyway, Anne told us he was only here in town for a visit, so I didn't much care if he didn't like it.

"I've got chores going wanting while you sit there eating that pie."

I wasn't lying. Cornell was playing the little ditty that meant he wanted a smoke.

Jimmy smiled. "You're a sharp-tongued one, kid. You remind me of myself when I was your age." I doubted Jimmy was ever like me, easygoing as he was. And for sure he was always white. "Seems Lil's pretty busy even for a Friday night."

"There's men with business in town staying at the hotel by the pier. Came in on the first ferry. I'm not sure what other business they've got, but they herded in here around eight-thirty."

Jimmy took another bite and rolled his eyes at Margaret. Her pie was all right, but not worth that fuss. She beamed at him. That's the way he was. He forked another piece. A chunk of strawberry got caught on his mustache.

"I guess that policeman didn't notice they were here," he said.

Officer Hickman had been sitting in that same chair when Miss Lil's first visitors came in earlier. He never even got off his duff to go check them out.

"You know the mayor takes care of Miss Lil."

"Indeed I do, kid." He lifted the mug of coffee as if to salute her.

"I've got to go," I said. "I think the girls are coming down to the parlor."

Cornell's ragtime was getting more lively.

"Anne told me you'd go by the bank today."

He said it like I hadn't said anything about being busy. Margaret fluttered around him. She offered him another slice and he smiled and shook his head. Instead, she refilled his cup.

"I dropped it off. Gave it to old man Evans."

Sometimes one or two of the girls had me drop off their pay at the bank. None of them—outside of Miss Lil—were made to feel welcome in town. The towners tolerated me more than they did them as long as I kept my place. Anne had asked me to take an envelope in there for Jimmy.

He looked at me. "I told Anne it should go to this Mr. Dodson to put in his bank."

"I didn't go in the bank. They've got rules about who can do that. Don't worry though. She sealed it up."

I didn't know what was in Jimmy's envelope. Likely it was money, but it was too thin and flat to hold much.

I never saw him want for anything, but he never worked that I could see. He must have paid Miss Lil for Anne's time, because he spent most nights up in her bedroom when we weren't busy. I couldn't figure why Miss Lil would allow that unless he bought her time up. If that was so, Miss Lil must have kept his money aside. It never showed up when I worked the books for her.

"If you're worried about it, why didn't you take it down yourself?"

He smiled at me. "Because I thought your girlfriend's daddy would make an exception for you."

I was so surprised at that I almost didn't get my words out.

"What do you know about it? She's not my girlfriend. And I've never talked to her father."

"I'm sorry, kid. Don't get excited. I've been told you're sweet on her."

I felt my face flush.

"I've got to go."

I didn't want to hear anymore from him. I left him with Margaret and went into the parlor to relieve Cornell. I worried about what Anne had said to Jimmy. Anne was the nearest thing I had to a friend back then, but I hadn't said much to her about Hannah, except seeing her in town at the July Fourth doings the year before. Now I'd have to wait until the next morning to find out what she told him.

3

Last July, like every year on the Fourth, Lewes Town held a shindig in the middle of Second Street. They had sack races and an egg toss and contests to see who could eat a pie the fastest. They even handed out hot dogs and soda pop. It was one of the times that colored and even Nanticoke could take part in things the whites did.

My Ma used to take me in there when I was small, but I hadn't been back since. For some reason, the year after I started at Miss Lil's, I got it in my head to go again, maybe because she lived so close. I must have said something to her because she saw to it I was free that day. Of course, the street games were mostly for the kids, but I liked the free food and watching white folks act foolish and stopping over on the beach for the fireworks on the way home.

It was hot that day as usual, so I was standing under a big elm tree drinking root beer and taking it all in when somebody tapped me on the shoulder.

"Hello," a voice said.

I turned around, ready to chase off whoever decided to bother me. But no words came out. A girl with skin the color of vanilla ice cream stood behind me. She had on a buttoned-up pink dress and long white stockings, and she had brown hair tied up around her head. I could tell by her sly smile, or because of the way her blouse pushed out, that she was a little older than me, maybe fifteen or sixteen. She was beautiful, too beautiful to be talking to me, and too brazen for her own good. It wasn't common back then for whites to mix with the colored, and most whites didn't see us as any different from Negroes.

My arm jerked when she touched it. She giggled at that.

"My goodness. I won't bite. What's your name?"

"Sonny." I said it so softly I wasn't sure if she'd heard.

"Oh, he speaks. You don't look sunny to me. My name's Hannah. Do you smile, Sunny, or is mumbling all you do?"

It felt hot where she'd touched my arm. Her teasing eased my shakes a little, but I still looked around to see if anybody was watching.

"Should you be talking to me like this?"

"It's the only way I know how to talk. I'm sorry, Mr. Sunny, but I don't speak Indian."

"That's not what I meant…"

"I know what you meant."

She took hold of my hand with both of hers to show me she was still teasing. I tried to pull away, but she laced her arm inside mine.

"What are you so worried about?"

"Maybe you should be. Some people don't take well to seeing a white girl with an Indian."

"Some people don't take to castor oil, but that doesn't mean it's bad for you."

I wasn't sure it was good to be likened to medicine, but she seemed to think so. Still, her acting bold wouldn't help much if a white came over.

"Anyway, we're not Indian and white now. We're Hannah and Not So Sunny."

She relaxed her hold a little but kept her hands around my arm. I could have pulled away if I wanted to, but I found out I didn't. I looked around a third time and she laughed at me.

"Come on. It's a new century. Can't a girl do what she wants?"

No. She can't—at least not with an Indian.

"What do you want?" I asked.

"A smile for one thing. You can't go around being sour all the time, can you?"

I didn't smile. I tried staring at her instead.

"Why are you doing this?

Her turtle green eyes staring back made me look down. She leaned away a little, bracing herself on my arm, and tilted her head.

"Because you're interesting."

She slipped her hands along my arm and turned me around so I had to face her.

"What does that mean?"

"Interesting. Don't Indians have a word for that?" All this time she was smiling. "You're tall for one thing, you've got hair black as a horse's mane, and your skin's the color of bark. That's interesting."

I wondered if she could see my bark turning red. *Interesting?* Most whites were only interested in making me keep my place.

"I've got to go."

"I've got to. Not I got to. You're educated too. See? Interesting."

I didn't know what to make of her. The teachers at the Carlisle school had worked on my grammar as hard as they did my religion. That's why I ran away.

"I just don't think…"

"Maybe you shouldn't think. What with all the talking and smiling, it might be too much for you. Let's do the three-legged race."

"Three-legged race…?"

"You know, they tie our legs together and we race other people."

"I know what a three-legged race is. I just don't want to."

"Sure you do," she said and squeezed my arm. Her hands were soft as new bread. "Come on. I'll do the thinking." I let her tug me along.

"I don't think folks will like it. What if your father sees us together?"

"My father's away."

Imagining her home by herself made me shiver.

"What if somebody tells him?"

"Oh, they won't say much, not as long as they need what's in his bank."

"His bank?"

"He's the vice president."

"And he won't care?"

"I didn't say that. I said people won't tell him."

I shook my head. I didn't know why she picked on me or why she was sure her father wouldn't find out, but I settled for the answers I already had. I was so eager to be around her by then I didn't need as much urging as I should have.

We stepped up to the start line. The town fireman running the event looked confused at first, like he thought one of us had made a mistake. Then he saw her holding my hand and frowned and scowled. She smiled at him like he was an old uncle and called him by his name. He nodded a bit, not liking it, and never looked at me. He handed her a strip of white cloth and went down the line and tied other people's legs together, leaving us to do it for ourselves. Maybe people were afraid of her father. She handed me the cloth.

"Tie us up."

"Me?"

"I can't bend over in this skirt. Tie one end to my left ankle and the other to your right."

The thought of being down near her leg, let alone touching her ankle, made me wobbly. But I took the cloth and knelt on one knee. I started to tie the cloth to my leg, but she stopped me.

"You have to do me first. Otherwise you'll pull me over trying to tie me to you."

"Oh."

I shifted around so my nose was only a couple of inches from her skirt. I had trouble holding onto the strip and I dropped it —twice.

"Come on. They're about to start."

I held my breath and put a hand between her legs so I could reach around for the cloth. I tied a half-hearted loop.

"Tighter. I don't want it coming off."

I looped the cloth around a second time and tucked it in as tight as I could make myself. She tugged on it with her leg to test it and seemed happy. I tied my ankle to hers and then stood up and swung around so we were facing the same way and so she couldn't see my face. She wrapped her arm around mine and pulled me close enough to her that the crown of her head rested on my cheek. Her hair smelled like wildflowers and I could feel the press of her blouse on my ribs. If the man hadn't yelled, "Go," I might have fallen over.

I don't think we won the race. All I remember is her leg rubbing against mine as we hobbled down the street. And that it was over too fast. When we crossed over the painted line, she laughed and turned and hugged me. I laughed too, panting like a hound and sweating enough to fill a river. A few white kids clapped when we crossed the finish line, and a white mother scolded her daughter for doing it.

We tried the pie-eating contest next. We held our hands behind our backs and pushed our faces into the custard filling and gobbled. Some skinny kid ate four pies before either of us finished one. Hannah pointed to a rain barrel. We made our own contest of washing custard off us.

After that, we drank another pop while some old soldiers marched by with flags. Later, there were more sack races, and then we walked together over to the beach, where we sat in the sand underneath the pier so we could be alone together, and waited for it to be dark.

It was a wonderful but very strange day. I didn't figure out until much later what she was up to. But even knowing there might be hell to pay for it made it more exciting. Of course, she was wrong about people talking. Or about her father not finding out. It turned out nothing we did that day came free.

4

Anne was twenty-two. She wasn't the oldest of Miss Lil's girls, but she was the most grown up. She was the only one who wasn't from around here. She'd seen more of the world than what was squeezed between the bays. She acted the same around everyone, whether white or Negro or Indian. She knew I worked hard for my keep and she often thanked me for cleaning her room after she'd used it. And when you talked to her, she listened. She didn't look like she was thinking about what else she had to do.

I always thought of her as my big sister though I never had one, so I'm not sure exactly what that's like. Because of her I got the job with Miss Lil. She'd seen me sweating over a few days' work I got scraping barnacles off the pier. I guess she was impressed by how hard I worked because she spoke to Miss Lil about me. Miss Lil's repairman had quit, so she asked if I wanted his job, which I did. And that was that.

Anne and I hit it off right from the start, I guess like brother and sister. I don't know why. Maybe we both needed someone to talk to. She was comely like all of Miss Lil's girls, so it was more complicated in a way. I couldn't help sometimes noticing how comely she was and getting embarrassed at how I acted around her. But she always listened to me, and she tried to see things the way I did even when she thought I was wrong-headed. She spoke to me like I was grown up—Miss Lil did too—which made it easy to talk to her. I trusted Anne as much as anyone, even more than my brother.

By the time she got up the next morning, I'd polished all the furniture in the parlor waiting for her. Miss Lil made up the room to look like the lobby of a fancy hotel so the men who visited would feel we were high class. But that meant a lot to dust. I'd moved from outside repairs to doing whatever needed done. I got paid a dollar a week plus room and board. Miss Lil fixed me a cot in the storage room off the kitchen. When she found out I could keep record books—something I thank Carlisle for—she had me help with that sometimes, which wasn't something people trusted Indians with back then.

By the time Anne came down, I'd probably polished every bit of wood in that parlor twice. Pink and white squares colored her dress like a checkerboard. Her hair was pulled back and tied with a ribbon, except for one lock that had come loose. Her face was the shape of an oyster pearl and as fair-toned. Her eyes were brown like her hair, and her nose had a perfect point to it. She brought a plate of strawberries from the kitchen and pulled up a chair and sat down. I sat down too.

"I'm sorry I made you wait."

I meant to ask her about the money Jimmy gave her, but by that time I'd waited so long to talk about Hannah I forgot to. I went right to it.

"How did you find out about Hannah?"

"What?" She looked surprised at my blurting it out. I could see I wasn't making any sense.

"Jimmy said you told him about us…about her."

"Hannah? Oh, is that the banker's daughter?" She poked at a strawberry with her fork and thought about it. "You told me about her, I think." I was sure that wasn't so and she saw me frown. "No, I take that back. I saw you together a few weeks back. From the smile on your face, it could have been your birthday."

I'm sure my face turned as red as the sofa. "You saw us?" Since that July Fourth, we'd only been together once.

She laughed a little. "Walking on the beach. You looked happy as a puppy."

I didn't know anyone had seen us that day, but I probably didn't look around carefully enough. Nothing I did that day was sensible. I wondered how long she'd watched us.

"Why did you tell Jimmy about it?"

Her doing that felt like she'd given away something that was mine. They probably had a good laugh over it.

"I wouldn't tell him those things, Sonny. That's your affair. Maybe Margaret said something to him. She looks for any reason to talk to him."

I looked at her. "Margaret? How would she know…?"

"Oh, my. I'm so sorry to surprise you like this, but it's not a secret. Everyone knows. It was nice that day. Emily and I went walking and Margaret came with us. We saw you two walking and we thought you looked cute together."

Everyone knows? I slumped down in the chair and stared at my knees. Anne saw I was embarrassed.

"Sonny, what's going on here? What about her?"

I raised my eyes but not my head. "She's not talking to me anymore. I think she's mad at me."

She pursed her lips. "What happened?"

"That's just it. I don't know. We were fine before, but now she's keeping away from me."

"Maybe she's busy. You don't get much time off, so you can't expect her to jump when you do."

I shook my head. "It's more than that, Anne. I used to walk with her when she was coming home from school when I could, but now she takes a different way."

"Did something happen? Did you say something she didn't like?"

"No." I said it a little too fast.

"Well, maybe she's found someone new."

My heart sank. I'd worried about that, but Anne saying it out loud made it seem certain.

"Do you think that's what it is, Anne? She's got another beau? One of those white boys at her school?"

"Maybe. Or maybe her daddy found out about you and made her stop."

If that was so, it was worse. If he found out about us, he might do a lot more than that.

"That would be bad," I said.

Anne nodded. "I know."

"How do I find out?"

"You already know what you need to do, Sonny. The way she's behaving, she's telling you not to come around anymore."

"But I want to know what happened. And I need to know she's all right."

Anne sat back in the chair. "I don't think that's a good idea. You know how town people feel about whites mixing. She's the banker's daughter, for heaven's sake. Is there anything else that might have made her act like this?"

"I don't know."

I guess because I lowered my eyes again, she knew I had some idea.

"Can you guess?"

That was one of the things I liked about her. She knew when I wasn't being honest, but she didn't call me out on it. I sat there a bit and then took a deep breath.

"I did something wrong, Anne. Very wrong."

"What?"

"I…I brought her in here."

Anne blinked. "In here? Into Miss Lil's? When?"

"The day you saw us."

"Oh, Sonny. What happened? Why would you do that?"

I didn't say anything, and she let me think about it. Then she said, "Tell me."

"She asked me to."

"Asked you? Why? Did the two of you…?"

"No. We didn't. She just wanted to look around upstairs. I don't know what she expected to find there. I waited for her to finish and then we went back outside. She didn't say anything after that. She just waved me away and went back into town. I could see she was troubled. I don't know what that was all about. Anne, please don't tell Miss Lil."

She shook her head slowly as if she was trying to make sense of it all.

"I'm going to have to tell her before someone else does, Sonny. Was anyone else in the house then?"

"No. Just me and her. I made sure about that."

"Okay. But go talk to her and find what she wanted up there."

"I will, Anne," I said. "I promise."

5

Some years ago, the railroad built a spur over the creek. It went out across the marsh to the beach and right up to the end of the Iron Pier. I guess it was so tourists just passing through wouldn't need to transfer into carriages in town. The train never got much use and the railroad went broke, but the tracks were still there and they made a shortcut for me to get from Miss Lil's house into town.

I was on the rail bed walking toward the wooden trestle bridge over the creek that'd bring me in just east of town. As I got near it, I was surprised to see my brother coming across the other way. From a distance at least, he looked sober.

Daniel hardly ever came to town. When he did, he didn't cover the ten miles there on foot. He looked as surprised as I was at first, but then he waved at me and walked out on the span.

"Hullo, Russell," he called.

I hate that name. It's the one the Carlisle Indian Industrial School gave me. I guess they thought it sounded Christian, though I never understood the connection. I was made to answer to it the two years I was in there.

"Hello, Daniel."

His Nanticoke name was Dntalemuns, which Ma said means my

little cat or something like that, and he hated it as much as I hated Russell. Most of his friends just settled for Daniel, which he didn't like much either, being a white name. But he let it go for lack of anything better.

I started to ask him how he was, but it was past noon and I thought I'd wait to be sure he wasn't drinking. As he got closer, I saw he was fine. He was bare-chested and wasn't wearing shoes. All he had on was a pair of canvas work trousers. His eyes were clear and he walked steady.

I pushed my fingers through my hair and tucked it over my shoulders.

"How are you, ni'mat?" I asked him. It was one of the other words Ma knew. It meant brother.

"What're you doing out here, Russell?" he asked me as he came up, using that name again.

I started to tell him not to call me that, but I knew he was just working on me. My given name is Senihele, which means sparrow hawk in Nanticoke. But town whites could only manage Sonny, which was okay too. After I came back from Carlisle, Daniel never called me by my Nanticoke name or even Sonny. From then on, I was just Russell to him. He said the Indian school had turned me white, so a white name fit me.

"On an errand," I said, trying not to look aggravated. "How about you?"

He was eight years older than me and about as tall. With his long black hair and dark eyes, he looked more Indian than I did. He wore his hair long too, longer than mine. He pretended to notice something on the tracks where he was walking and didn't answer me.

"Haven't seen you in weeks," I said. "You hanging around in town today?

It couldn't be a good thing finding him sneaking across the marsh, but who was I to talk? I wondered where he'd tied up his horse. He stopped in front of me and crossed his arms.

"I got a job."

He was sober and working. That was a big change. His feet were dirty from walking barefoot, but otherwise he looked like he'd cleaned up.

"That's good."

I said it before I could catch myself. His face tightened up.

"I guess I'll keep it then, now that I know it's okay with you."

"That's not what I mean. Come on, Daniel. Don't be like that." I felt my voice strain. "We hardly get to talk anymore."

Now he pretended to be surprised that he'd provoked me. I kept still and looked at him. Finally, he unfolded his arms and dropped his hands to his sides. His face lost some of its sour look.

"So we don't, brother. So let's talk. What's your errand?"

Our questions were going in circles, so I decided to give him an answer.

"Miss Lil asked me to pick up a few things in town and have some foodstuffs sent out from Maull's Grocery."

"Oh, she sends her houseboy now. Why didn't she go herself? She's got that fancy carriage."

"She's busy," I said, and this time I looked away.

"She's in trouble with the police, ain't she? Some nosy towner complained again, so she has to lay low."

"No. She's just busy."

I didn't tell him I was using the excuse so I could try to see Hannah.

Daniel laughed. "You think 'cause you went to white school those townies are going to sell you anything? You're just another colored to them, Russell. Lil should have sent one of her girls. They'll talk to a whore any day before they will you."

He was wrong about that part at least. I decided to talk about something else.

"Yeah. Maybe you're right. What about your job? What they got you doing?" What kind of work had him out walking the tracks instead of in town?

"Can't say much about it."

"Why not? It's work. Any job that pays is something, isn't it?" I hoped he wouldn't get mad again. "That's what you used to tell me."

"Pay's fine." He gave me a look. "But part of the job is not talking about it."

"Oh."

That couldn't be good either. I shut my mouth, not knowing what else to say, and we stared at each other a bit. Finally, he shrugged and clapped me on the shoulder. It was almost a friendly pat.

"I got to be going."

He nodded and with no more fuss he stepped past me and started down the rail bed. I turned around as he went by.

"Wait…"

He stopped and looked back.

"How much are you going to be in town? Maybe we can meet somewhere."

He laughed again, sounding almost likable this time. A long curl of his hair worked loose.

"Well, you're the one working at the bawdy house, Russell. You know I ain't welcome there, so I guess you'll have to come out to the cabin."

"I don't get off much, and I don't have use of a horse."

"Then I guess we're stuck, ain't we?"

"But if your job's in town…?"

"I didn't say it was, and you don't need to keep asking about it."

"Why not? Is it something that'll get you in trouble?"

"You ain't my Pa, Russell. That one's long dead." I'd set him on edge again, and I didn't dare come back at him on it. He seemed to think about what to say next. "At least I ain't running some townie's errands—or a whore's either." He grinned at me, but now there was spite in it. He gave me a look that meant figure that one out and then started off toward the beach.

"Daniel."

He didn't turn around this time. I called after him again, but he kept on walking. Our talk was finished. I watched him go and wondered what to make of it. If he had a job he couldn't talk about, the only thing I could think of was trouble. And after not running into him in so long, all we could do was throw words at each other.

He crossed the salt marsh and disappeared into the woods. I stood there a while longer. Then I turned around and headed for town. Now it wasn't just about seeing Hannah or even doing chores for Miss Lil. I also wanted to find out what Daniel had gotten himself into. I owed him that, even if he didn't like it. He'd saved me a couple of times by then and I hadn't had the chance to pay him back.

I turned around, crossed over the trestle bridge and headed toward town.

6

It hadn't always been like that with us. Before I got sent up to Carlisle, Daniel acted better toward me. And later on too, right after he got me out of that place.

When Pa died, the county sheriff made my mother send me to Indian school in Pennsylvania. He wanted to send Daniel, but he was too old by then and our Ma begged to let him stay to help with the farm. Not that it did her much good. In little more than two years, she was dead from coughing sickness. It was the winter of my second year when Daniel got word to me that our Mother was sick. I asked the school for leave to go see her, but the preacher in charge wouldn't give it. He said she'd likely be in the ground before I got home anyway, and there was no point in my going.

I hated the Carlisle school from the start. There was nothing up there to do but learn what Christians thought I should know and follow rules. They had a lot of them. Rules for studying and working and eating and sleeping and even using the outhouse. And if we didn't heed them exactly the way they told us, our punishment was a whipping with a fat belt. At least that was to my seat rather than my arms so I didn't have to walk around all black and blue up there too. And we could only talk English up there, never Indian. Since I didn't know much Nanticoke—my grandmother was the last one who spoke it at home—that part was no problem for me. But some boys from the northern tribes had only ever spoke in their own tongues, so they had to just stay quiet until they learned enough white language to get by.

After being free to do what I liked at home, at least when Pa was away, all their rules and whippings and the teachers droning about Jesus and George Washington and white man's history were enough to make me crazy. So I caught onto things pretty quickly and learned how to get my way up there. I worked hard at my chores without complaining and I pretended to be excited about learning Christian ways.

But that day I asked the preacher for leave to go see my dying mother and he wouldn't allow it marked the end of my pretending.

I stopped studying and wouldn't even put a mark on the tests they handed out. I played a ragtime ditty during Sunday service once and that ended my piano playing. And I got into a lot of fights after that, each of which earned me a week in the school jail. By then I didn't care. It wasn't a real jail, just an old stable out back with a padlock on the door, but it served the purpose.

One night while I was locked in there with a supper of cold chicken and hard bread they'd brought me, one of the bars screwed across the stable window started rattling, which scared me half to death.

"You in there?" somebody outside asked.

I didn't answer. The handyman who'd brought my food before was long gone. I didn't know if the person was talking to me or just passing by and decided to goad me. I stood up, though, and went over to the window. Whoever it was outside grabbed the bar and shook it a second time.

"Hey," he said, louder this time, and I knew that voice. I looked out though the iron bars. Enough light remained for me to see it was Daniel, and he looked at me, provoked.

"Why didn't you answer me?"

"What are you doing up here?"

He sat astride a huge brown horse. It chuffed when I showed my face at the window and tried to back away, but Daniel steadied it with his heels. He was riding it bareback.

"What are you doing in there, Russell?"

"I don't…" Seeing my brother there right outside made me lose my tongue for a bit. "I was fighting," I managed to get out.

"Fightin' "? They got you locked up in a barn for that. What'd you do? Hit a preacher?"

"No. A Mohawk kid. What are you doing here?" I asked him again.

"They put you there for fighting with an Indian? Christians are crazy. You know that?"

I did.

"Why are we talking about that, Daniel? What are you doing out there?"

"Someone up at the school told me you were out here. I came up to tell you that Ma died."

Even though I'd half-expected it, the news hit me hard. "When…?"

"Couple of weeks ago. I had someone write and tell you she was sick, but you didn't answer. She was real bad near the end. She wanted to see you."

"I tried to come home, but they wouldn't let me." It was like something had grabbed the insides of my chest.

"After I wrote you, she held on for a couple of weeks. You would've had time."

"I wanted to come. What killed her?"

He shook his head. "Doctor said it was coughing sickness. He only came out to see her one time."

"I'm sorry," I said, meaning for a lot of things.

"Yeah well, I guess that doesn't matter now." His voice changed then like he didn't want to talk anymore about it. "So you want to stay in there or you wanna go home?"

"Home? They won't let me do that."

He looked off to the side at something and then back at me.

"Sit still. I'll be right back."

Like I had somewhere else to go. He clucked at the horse and turned away. I watched him until he was out of sight around the barn and wondered how he got there. The school was over a hundred miles from where we lived, and that plow horse didn't look fit enough to have come that far. It hadn't even worked up a lather. I stewed about it a couple of minutes and then the padlock on the outside of the stable door started to clatter.

"Stand back a bit," Daniel whispered at me through a crack in the door.

"What are you going to do?"

"Just get back."

His voice trailed off then, and he moved away from the door. The lock kept on rattling. Whatever he was planning, the supervisor wouldn't be happy about it. My stomach turned over. Then the door lurched and bent outward and boards splintered. I jumped backward a couple of steps.

"Don't," I shouted, though why I don't know. I was scared, I guess.

The hinges broke loose and the door exploded out and away like it'd been struck with a sledgehammer. The door shattered into jagged, wooden icicles that went flying with a sound like a thunderbolt. I'm sure they could hear it inside the school buildings. Where the stable door used to be, a large ragged hole looked out on a slice of darkened farmland. Daniel was twenty feet from me, still on the horse, whose tail pointed toward me. He twisted himself around on its back and started coiling a long rope he was holding. As he wound it up, the other end dragged a bent-up iron latch that went bumping over the dirt, heading for the horse's rear end.

"What are you standing there for?" he yelled at me. "Get your ass moving."

I moved. "What are we doing?"

The back porch of the nearest school building was fifty yards further on past us. Lights went on up there and I could hear voices.

"If you don't get up here now, we ain't going nowhere."

I ran to the horse and raised my arm. He grabbed it and lifted me up behind him. I wrapped my arms around him, and he wheeled the horse around, heading away from the school. That plow horse was livelier than I'd thought. Daniel got it moving at a pretty fast trot. I twisted back and saw people milling on the back porch like stirred up bees. With dark settling in, it didn't look like they'd figured out where the noise came from. We were through the back gate and into the woods behind the school before they did.

"Where'd you get the horse?" I shouted in his ear.

"Borrowed it."

Borrowed it? More likely some farmer would wake up minus an animal in the morning.

"This plow horse can't get us home. How'd you get up here?"

"Train."

"Train?" The pieces got clear to me. "Took you some time then."

"Not much." Then he added, "Ma never wanted you up here."

"I didn't have a say in it. Did she suffer much, Daniel?"

"Maybe. Don't know for certain. She cried a lot, but the fever put her out of her head. I don't think she knew anything."

I didn't have anything else to say. We rode without talking much for a bit.

"You're better off out of there," he said after a while. "Can't learn nothing from whites except how to be white."

"Uh-huh," I said. They tried hard at doing that.

The Carlisle Indian school was only a couple of miles from some train tracks and that's where we headed. He shooed the horse off. I hope it found its way home again. We slept beneath a trestle bridge that night. I kept waking up, though, half expecting the supervisor to be standing over me with his belt. The next morning, we hopped onto a passing boxcar when the train slowed for the bridge. A hobo sleeping in there didn't give us any trouble.

That's how we got home, and it turned into a great adventure for us. We laughed about how we put one over on the Indian school, and we talked about our good times with Ma and grumbled about the ones with Pa. We rode on that way for two days and a night, changing trains here and there, until we jumped off the last one just outside Millsboro.

We stayed out at the farm together that spring. I did some

planting and helped Daniel with the livestock we had left. We drank coffee on the porch together in the mornings. At night when Daniel went into town, I sat by myself and sometimes cried about Ma. I didn't go to town for fear someone from the Indian school would come looking for me. But they never did. Those two months with Daniel were the best we'd ever had together. We acted more like brothers then than at any time before or since.

That was the second time Daniel saved me, and I hadn't yet paid him back for the first. That other one happened when I was ten years old, living with Ma and Pa and him in our cabin out in the country where other Nanticoke lived. It's what got me sent to Carlisle.

Each year back then, I used to mark the days until planting season started because Pa stayed at home then and worked the fields. He'd wear himself out doing it and flop into bed right after supper. But during winter, there wasn't much of farming, so he worked days at Houston's Sawmill. That should have worn him out too, except he'd stop at a tavern after work every night and come home drunk, mean and spoiling to fight. He'd start in on Ma, making up reasons to yell at her, and then I'd start crying and he'd take a switch to me. I'd try to hide under our table, but he'd come after me with a shovel or the butt of his shotgun. In those days, my hands stayed swollen and purple from covering my face. Most mornings, I'd go to the Mission School with bruises and knots on both arms. The Methodist teachers never said much about it, though. I guess they knew about Pa's nasty side.

Daniel sometimes had jobs then, so he wasn't always home. When he did catch Pa waling on me, he'd try to wrestle him off. He caught his own hell for that. As Daniel got older, though, he got strong enough to push Pa out the door, which wasn't hard since Pa was already staggering. Daniel would lock him out there all night to sleep off his drunk. Next day nothing much was said about it. I think Pa was sort of scared of him by then. But by evening it would start in again.

Then one night, Pa came home and his fists and a shovel weren't enough. Something disagreeable must have got into him that day because he was even more out of sorts than usual. As soon as he came in the door, he went after Ma because dinner wasn't ready. He usually slapped her and saved his punches for me. But not that time. I was a little older by then and I sassed him for it. Of course, he turned on me. Daniel wasn't home, so it was just him and me.

Like I said, I was around ten, but I put up my fists and dared him to hit me. He cursed at me and called me the butcher's bastard and I yelled back at him that I wished I was. His face got red and he grabbed an iron poker and swung it at me. I didn't get my hands up and it caught the side of my face near my eye and I went down on my knees. He pulled back for another swing and I put up my arms and he hit them so hard he cracked my wrist. I dropped all the way to the floor and clawed under the table with my good hand.

Ma screamed for him to stop, but he paid no attention. He kicked the table away and spread his feet and lifted the poker with both hands. He would have killed me, but Daniel came in and yanked the poker away. Pa was so surprised he yelped and spun around to see who'd done that to him. Daniel held the poker tight and stood his ground, staring at Pa like he'd use it on him. Pa knew he could. Daniel was eighteen then and strong as a bull, so Pa went for the iron skillet on the stove.

He was half-turned away when Daniel swung the poker—hard—at the side of Pa's head. Pa stopped roaring and started to gurgle. He dropped the skillet, went to his knees and fell on his face. Then he crumpled up like dirty laundry.

Everything got quiet. Ma stood still with her hands to her face, staring down at Pa like she expected him to get up and come at her. Daniel held the poker a little off the floor like he expected the same thing. I was bleeding and numb, but I knew better. Blood spurted from Pa's head like his meanness had come unstopped.

Daniel got an old blanket and had me help him roll Pa up in it. He told Ma we were going out a bit. He had to say it twice before she looked at him. Daniel took one end of the blanket and I took the other under my good arm. We dragged Pa outside and pushed and pulled him over the back of our horse. It was a dead winter night and Houston's mill stream was only a couple of miles from our cabin. Daniel used the sharp end of the poker to knock a big hole in the ice. We rolled Pa into the water and Daniel tossed the poker in after him. Later on, we burned the blanket in our wood stove. Ma couldn't watch us do it.

The sheriff came out next morning to tell us Pa had been found out at the mill under the ice. Ma couldn't talk to him. He took that to mean the news distressed her and he said how sorry he was. He asked Daniel if he knew anything, but Daniel said Pa never made it home. He asked what happened to me and I told him I got into a fight at school. I don't think he believed any of it, but he wrote it up as an accident. He didn't have the time or interest to find out how a drunken Indian had gotten himself killed.

The sheriff wasted no time getting me sent off to the school at Carlisle. Ma was miserable with grieving and she went half-crazy begging him not to do it. But he did anyway. Like I said, he let Daniel stay back to run the farm.

The morning the sheriff came to tell us Pa died, Daniel had never looked surprised or sorry, which put the sheriff off on him, I think. Daniel was always a little wild, but he got worse after Pa died. The sheriff hounded him every chance he got from then on. He couldn't credit a son not mourning his pa. I guess his own pa was a different sort than ours.

I still remember standing on the ice at the mill run. It must have been cold and my face was bleeding, but I couldn't feel any of it. The last I saw Pa, his lips were purple, his face swollen up and the side of his head caved in. I had no more feeling for him then than I would a slaughtered hog. I still don't. I owed Daniel.

I was determined to keep him from buying trouble even if he was hell-bent on it.

7

I crossed over the trestle bridge and followed the farm road that ran beside the creek into town. The creek's water was brackish—not fit to drink—and was more of an inlet of the bay than a proper stream. It spanned the length of town, separating the beach area from the town proper, and the locals liked it fine that way. Though things boomed in those days with the ocean trade, the breakwater contractors, the train commerce, the fishing fleets and the visitors, all of that was quarantined on the bayside. The creek insured that any disreputable types who passed time at the beach wouldn't soil the city folks.

I stopped at the end of Second Street to look for colored faces. Everyone was white, and none of them gave me as much as a glance. It was still early but the town was wide awake. The stores were open and busy. Fresh bread at Fitzsimmon's Bakery and fresh droppings from Hopkins stables crowded the air. Towners might not have much use for beach folks, but every one of them got up early to do business with them. I didn't see the old man, which was good. He was likely staying at one of the hotels on the beach. But no one I was friendly with was hanging about there either.

I decided to seek out Johnny Norwood, a Negro boy I sometimes fished with. He could have heard something about the old man. He had a job stocking goods at Maull's and he was always ready to share any white gossip he'd overhead there. I couldn't go in the front door, of course, but I could get to the storeroom where Johnny worked by going around back.

I stepped up onto the sidewalk and started down the block. My route took me right past the bank and I slowed down as I went by. I made a show of looking at the jobs list pasted in the front window. I peered through the glass at the tellers behind the counter, seeing if I could figure out which one was Hannah's father. Instead, I saw Hannah.

She was folded into a hardback chair with her knees tucked under her chin and her arms wrapped around her legs. Her lips were pressed closed and her face was blotchy. I tapped on the glass. She looked up at me, then jumped out of the chair as if she'd sprung from a jack-in-the-box. She started across the lobby, almost running, pushing through a line of people to get away from me. I shifted over to the bank's door and pulled it open.

"Hannah, I need to talk to you," I shouted.

"Go away," she shouted back, sounding angry and scared.

Evans, the bank guard, caught my shirt sleeve and twisted me back out the door. "No colored allowed inside."

Hannah stopped running, looking like she wasn't sure where to go. Then she spun around and came back my way.

"Hannah."

"Go away."

She pushed her way out from behind Old Man Evans and went flying past me. Her hand brushed against me as she went. Someone from inside the bank called after her, but she didn't turn around. She started up the street in a run and I started after her.

"Hannah, what's wrong?"

She yelled at me over her shoulder. "Don't talk to me." She was crying now too.

"Why? What did I do?"

An old colored man passing by gave me a dirty look. Hannah

was running hard now—in that toes-in way girls do—and she didn't slow down. She shouted at me without looking back.

"Don't be stupid. Get out of here, Sonny."

Her words landed like punches. I slowed down, not sure what to do. It almost sounded like she was worried, like she was warning me or something. She was far down the street by then. A woman in a black dress coming around the corner heard Hannah shout. She put a glove to her mouth and frowned at me too.

I stopped. "Hannah?"

The pink dress disappeared around the corner of Market Street. Her house was three blocks down the street. If I took off running, I still might catch up with her before she got inside, but I didn't think it would do any good.

A wide paw grabbed my shoulder from behind.

"We need to talk, boy."

I thought it was Evans and tried to pull away, but the grip was strong. I spun around, squirming to get loose, and saw the old man's hard eyes staring at me from under his hat brim. Confused as I was at first, I thought Hannah was running away from him.

"Leave her alone," I said.

"You lied to me yesterday." His mustache bobbed as he talked

"Let go of me." I struggled but couldn't get loose of him.

"Not until you answer some questions."

"I can't answer your questions. I don't know what you're talking about." I twisted halfway around to get a look down the street. "Let me go."

I lashed out with my boot and landed a good one on his shin. He twitched but didn't make a sound, though it must have hurt like hell. He jerked me around again.

"Where's Ryan?"

"I don't know anybody by that name."

"But you know the man I mean. I saw it in your eyes yesterday."

In my eyes? I shrugged and tried to wriggle away.

"He's going by Lowe now." He saw me start to argue and pointed a finger at my face. "Don't waste my time, son. I know you know who he is. He frequents that house where you work."

I guess he'd asked around about Jimmy and found him. I was surprised anybody in town took notice of him.

"Since you already know everything, what do you want me for?"

"Where is he now?"

"I don't know, and I don't much care. I don't follow him around."

Another man's voice chimed in from behind us. "Stop right there, mister. We don't take to strangers manhandling folks."

The old man looked over his shoulder at the newcomer and I looked too. A tall man, skinny as a marsh weed, was right behind him. His black suit looked like it was sewn onto him, and his shoes were so polished he could use them to shave. His hair was cut short and slicked back and his cheeks were pasty-colored like he didn't see much sun. He was around forty, I guess, but his wormy frown and undersized glasses made him look starchy as a codger. He stopped glaring at the old man, looked at me, and his cheeks colored.

"Even colored trash," he said, like he meant to say more.

He looked down the street and then back at me. I knew then it was Hannah's father. He came out looking for her and saw the old guy roughing me up. I don't think he would've said anything if he'd known it was me. He stepped in closer to us, a little stiff-legged, like he had a war wound or something.

"You're Sockum." He said it like it was a curse, not a question. I didn't answer. "What are you doing around here?"

The old man turned to look at him. He didn't turn loose of me, and I got pulled around too.

"Who are you?" he asked Hannah's father.

"I'm not colored," I barked. "I'm Nanticoke."

I don't know if her father knew the difference or cared. He left off glowering at me and looked at the old man.

"I needn't answer to you, sir," he said, "but I'm Henry Dodson, vice president of National Bank."

He pulled himself up like a cock and gestured at the building. The old man looked at it. It was a plain wooden thing that looked more like a schoolhouse.

"Big title for a little bank. It have a president too?"

"Mr. Sippel lives out of town," Mr. Dodson said as if he'd been insulted. "I'm in charge here."

The old man thought about that a second or two. "Well, Mr. Dodson, if you're in charge, then we need to have a talk."

"Talk?" Dodson looked surprised. "Who do you think are you, sir?"

"I know who I am, Mr. Dodson." He pulled an odd-shaped metal badge from his vest pocket and held it up for Dodson to see. "I'm a U.S. Deputy Marshal, and if you're smart, you'll hear me out. It concerns this bank of yours."

Dodson's frown went worming around on his forehead. It looked like he didn't want to waste time talking to the old man, but I could see he was curious about what he had to say. He looked up the street again, thinking about his daughter, I guess, but then he nodded.

"All right, sir. Say your piece."

"Inside is better," the old man said.

Dodson stared at him but when he didn't offer him any more, he nodded a second time and extended his arm, pointing the way. The old man let go of me and started past him, walking toward the bank. Instead of following him, Dodson held back and his face drew up tight. The veins popped out on his skinny neck and he clenched his fists like he'd like to thrash me right there if he could get away with it.

"Now I know your face, Sockum."

That was bad.

The old man—the marshal—stopped walking and turned around too.

"Sockum," he said to me, "we ain't done yet." I didn't say anything to either one of them. "Ryan or Lowe, you see him, you tell him I'm here for him." He held my stare a second longer and then grunted and turned away.

Mr. Dodson let him go ahead and then pushed a bony finger to my eyes.

"You're going to pay, black boy. You understand me?"

I shook my head a little. "No, sir. I don't."

He looked like he wanted to say more, but a man came out of

the bank and smiled at him. Dodson nodded but after he passed by, he put his face close to mine and stretched his lips into a snarl.

"I'm coming for you now and I'll strip your hide off. You understand that, don't you?"

I nodded.

He straightened up, brushed at his coat with both hands and without saying anything else turned around and followed the old man into his bank.

Her father did know. I wondered if he'd seen us together, or if somebody told him. Strip my hide off? He wouldn't like his daughter mixing with me, but could he be that lathered up about us holding hands? But what else could he know? Only Hannah knew the other thing. No wonder she was in a commotion. What had he done to her? I thought about going to her house, but with her father onto us, she'd never come out.

How could the day have turned so miserable? I still hadn't done my shopping, and it wasn't even nine o'clock.

8

I was halfway back to Miss Lil's house with a bolt of fabric under my arm when I came across Jimmy going the other way. I didn't notice him at first. I was too busy thinking about Hannah and her father.

"Whatcha got there, kid? You makin' yourself a dress?"

I shaded my eyes against the low morning sun. He was wearing the same shirt from the night before, but his coat was gone now and he was riding one of the bicycles the Pavilion Hotel kept for its stay-over guests. I doubt he'd asked to use it. He waved as he went by me and rocked his front wheel back and forth too.

"Hey Jimmy. Is Anne up yet?" I called back at him.

"Up and into town already." He shaded his eyes too, steering with one hand. I never learned to ride a bike. It seemed a lot of trouble when you could just walk. "You came that way. Didn't you see her?" He braked and rounded to come back to me.

"No." I was disappointed and I'm sure I showed it. "Where was she going?"

"To the bank and some other places."

"The bank?" I stopped walking. "I just went by there. I didn't see her."

She could have been standing right in the lobby, though. I didn't notice anybody else after I saw Hannah in there. Jimmy rode around me in wide circles, churning out grooves in the sand as he went.

"She took the buggy. Left less than a half hour ago. She was probably stabling the mare when you came out of town. You must've just missed her."

"Darn it." The Christians at Carlisle had tried to clean up my coarse language, but it still worked on me now and then. "Why'd she go to the bank?"

"She's renting me a deposit box," he said.

That was strange. He'd be a sight more welcome in the bank than she would. Folks usually frowned on the girls being in town. I turned away and started walking again, though there was no need to rush if Anne wasn't there. He stopped going in circles and fell in beside me.

"Something wrong with you?"

"Why's she doing your chores?" I asked.

"Well, you can't do 'em. You said they wouldn't let you inside."

"I mean why don't you do them yourself? You don't look that busy."

"I got plenty to do, kid. What's eating at you anyway?"

"Nothing. What do you need a deposit box for?" I didn't need him asking about my business.

"The hotel where I'm staying doesn't have a safe. I've got some things need protecting."

"I thought you said you were just visiting. Why don't you give them to Miss Lil to keep for you?"

"Well, you're almost right," he said. "I ain't staying much longer. What she's putting in the bank is for her to keep."

"You said it was yours."

"It is. I'm giving it to her."

"Oh yeah? What is it?"

"Awful nosy, aren't you? How about you telling me your business first? Like what's bothering you, for instance?" His big-faced grin meant he was kidding mostly.

"You're giving her money?"

He suddenly took interest in the lighthouse out on the cape. I could see he was deciding how much to tell me, or what.

"Well, I've known her a long time. She helped me out more than once. Fortune's smiled on me since, so I thought I'd return the favor. I want her to put it away someplace safe until she can buy herself something. Jewelry maybe."

"She's got jewelry."

"Yeah, well now she can get more. And while she's there, she's also going to check if there are any jobs posted that might fit me."

This story sounded made-up too, but I was getting used to that about him.

"So if you got money and you're only visiting, why is she looking for jobs for you?"

"I guess she wants me to stay around longer is all. She's hoping I'll get some steady work and settle in for a bit."

"But that's not your plan, is it?"

"Oh, I'll stay a while. She's a persistent one. What with all the trade moving through town now, she thinks it's likely extra help is needed."

"You ever done any real work, Jimmy? You don't seem the type to me." I couldn't see him stamping mail.

He looked over at me but kept grinning. "As a matter of fact, I have. Lots of it. Ever worked on a ranch? That's backbreaking work."

"So I guess just now you were going into town to find a job just to keep her happy?" I knew he wasn't.

"You're a persistent bugger, ain't you? No. I was heading down to the Ocean House. I heard they have a faro game there in the evenings in the back."

"I thought you were staying there? I mean when you're not up in Anne's room. Don't you know what they have in back?" Like I said, I got smart-mouthed when I was aggravated.

"I stayed there last week," he said. "I'm at the Breakwater now. I figure to try out all the hotels while I'm here."

"That'll use up three nights. I guess Anne's room is good for the rest?"

He laughed out loud. "That's a good one. Anyway, last night some fella at the bar told me about the game. But he was far into his cups, so I decided I'd check it out myself."

"They have one at the Clubhouse," I said, meaning a run-down fishermen's bar up the beach past the Iron Pier. Daniel told me he used to stop in there now and then.

"Yeah well, maybe I'll check into it too."

I noticed he didn't ask me how to find it.

"Okay. Enough blabbing about me. What's up with you? Why you looking for Anne?"

"You ever heard of James Ryan?" I asked him.

"James Ryan? No. Can't say I have. Common enough name, though. What about him? Is he giving you trouble?"

I give him credit. He never so much as blinked.

"Some stranger—an old guy calling himself a U.S. Deputy Marshal—came to town yesterday looking for him. Seems to think I know something about it."

"Why would he think that?"

"He says this Ryan hangs out at houses and parlors. Thought I might have seen him."

"Huh. Have you?"

"Not that I know. From the way he described him, though, he sounds a bit like you."

Jimmy's laugh was a bray this time. "That's a good one coming from a kid who told me all white men look alike."

He started to laugh so hard he had to stop pedaling. I stopped and looked at him. What I'd said wasn't that funny.

"So you don't know him then?"

He snorted and shook his head. "I already said I didn't. This marshal say what he wants with him?"

"Nope. He just said if I see Ryan to tell him he's here for him. Don't know what he meant."

"Here for him? Don't seem very friendly, does he? What's he look like?"

"Like I said, he's old. He's a big man, though, and has a hard stare. There's not much humor in him. Talks funny too like he's not from around here."

"Well, the way you talk sounds funny to me, kid. He give you a name?" He pushed off and started peddling again.

"No."

"Where'd you see him?"

"Yesterday. On the pier, coming off the ferry. Again today down by the bank."

"The bank?"

"Yeah. After he finished with me, he went inside. You seem pretty interested in him for someone who knows nothing about it."

"I'm worried about you. I can see you're stirred up from meeting him."

We'd reached the front of Miss Lil's. I lifted the bolt of cotton and held it up. "I've got to get this inside."

"Okay. I gotta go anyway." He climbed off the bicycle, turned it around and got back on. "I see Anne I'll tell her you're looking for her." He waved and started off. "And if I run into your marshal, I'll tell him to leave you be. In fact, you go tell him I'm coming to see him and give him a piece of my mind. That ought to stir him up."

I shook my head, surprised he wanted to deal with the marshal face to face. That's something I'd like to see.

"Okay, I'll be sure to tell him."

"You do that." I watched him ride down the beach and I went inside.

9

Anne wasn't home. I had to talk to Hannah, especially because her father knew who I was. I left the fabric roll in the kitchen and went back outside. Crossing the creek at the railroad bridge brought me in near the east edge of town. I jumped down off the tracks and hurried across an open field on the outskirts.

After running into Daniel, I was leery about who else might be about. So I went into town a roundabout way—past the ice company to Third Street and then over toward Market. The houses there were all tall, free-standing soldiers, some a bit down at heel, with small lots in between them like spaces for veterans on parade. Only a few had first-floor stores, so the street wasn't nearly as busy as Second Street that time of day. If the marshal was still poking around, I hoped he wouldn't hang around there. It was early afternoon, so even though Hannah might be in school, as worked up as she was that morning I was hoping she'd decided not to go. I was only a few steps from her house when I saw her.

She was sitting on her porch on a wicker rocker. I stopped in my tracks, afraid she'd spot me and run inside. She sat there, folded up, with her legs tucked under her chin, looking down at the sidewalk through the railing slats. It was like she was lost in a fog. She wore the pink dress she had on at the bank, but tangles of her undone hair drooped to her shoulders. From the fresh blotches on her face, she'd been crying. I started to say something but caught myself. She hadn't noticed me, and if I startled her she might bolt. I walked past the porch slowly to see if she'd notice me and look up. She didn't, so I stopped and turned toward her.

"Hannah." I tried to keep my voice quiet.

She jolted upright like she'd been stung. Her eyes opened wide at first. But when she saw who it was, they softened a little, which surprised me. She started to say something but then decided not to. She looked around like she thought someone might be watching, but at least she didn't run inside. Maybe she wasn't as angry with me as I thought. I took a chance and rested my hand on the porch rail.

"Tell me what's wrong. Please."

She stared at me a couple of seconds and I thought she might say something. But then she shook her head and looked down. It seemed like she couldn't decide whether I should be there.

I tried again. "Hannah?"

She looked at me, then started to stand. She would go inside, and I didn't know what to say to keep her from it. As she got up, she glanced up the street again and stopped moving. I turned too, fearing her father might be coming. Instead, two girls were coming up the sidewalk from the direction of town.

They were Hannah's age—sixteen, I guess. One of them had hair the color of wet sand and the other's hair was black. Each wore the same pink dress Hannah had on, the uniform they had to wear at school. I think Hannah had pointed them out to me at the July Fourth doings, but I couldn't remember their names. The sandy-haired one waved at Hannah.

"Why weren't you in school today?" Her smile seemed a little fake, like she was mocking her.

"Maybe she's playing hooky with Sonny." The other girl was more plain-looking—big nose and fat eyebrows—but her hair was so black and shiny she might have had Indian blood. They both stared at Hannah and waited.

Hannah slumped back into the chair and crossed her arms in

front of her. "Well, I was sick, for your information." She might have been sick, but she was also acting as if she was embarrassed at my being there.

"Well, you don't look sick," the black-haired girl said. "You look like you've been crying, though. What happened? Did Sonny break your heart?"

Hannah looked down at her lap. "Just go away."

"Oh, so that is what happened." Sandy hair gave me a look like she'd caught me at something wicked.

"Why aren't you two in school?" I said to her, and I made it sound like I was scolding them.

The dark hair girl looked at me too. "Well, for your information, Sonny Sockum, we are. We only walked home for lunch, and if you were going to colored school instead of living at that house, you'd know very well what we're doing."

I stared them down like I might come after them, but the truth is they seemed silly to me. My life was filled with bigger problems. These two acted like their little jokes mattered. I wanted to shake their heads until their foolish brains fell out, which wouldn't take too long, but I just glared at them until one and then the other looked away.

Hannah looked at them and now there was fire in her eyes. "Both of you mind your business and leave me alone. And for your information, I'm going in later to get my homework. Not that it's any concern of yours." Sandy hair smirked, so she added, "And I'm not hanging out with Sonny. In fact, he's leaving now too." She gave me a sharp look.

"Okay, Hannah. Whatever you say." Black hair looked at her like she knew what she was really up to, and then she gave me a teasing smile to show me she knew about me too. I was tempted to reach over and smack her. Hannah glared at them. Sandy hair looked away but didn't lose the mocking in her voice.

"Well, we have to go now. I'm sure we'll see you at school later, Hannah—when you come to get your homework, I mean." She said it like she didn't believe a word of it. The black-haired girl flicked her fingers in a wave. "Goodbye, you two." Their faces were turned to each other, whispering and giggling, as they headed up the street in the direction of school. I heard one of them laugh. Hannah stared at their backs.

"They make me so mad." It was the first thing she'd said directly to me since I got there.

"Dumb girls," I said to give us something to agree about.

She put her hand on the rocker and moved it back and forth in her agitation. She waited until they were out of sight before she said anything else.

"You need to not be here."

"Why? What did I do?"

"My father's looking for you."

"Yeah. I already saw him. He came out of the bank after you left. He told me to stay away from you. Is that what you want too?"

She glanced down the sidewalk toward town, maybe afraid her father might be coming. He wasn't. "It's more than that," she said.

"More? What's more?"

"When he saw you downtown before, he didn't know everything," she said. "Everything that happened, I mean."

I felt the blood go cold in me. "Everything?"

"He's really mad now, Sonny." She looked down at her lap, not at me. "He told me he'd kill you."

"Kill me?" I looked down the street again. "Why? He didn't see us at Miss Lil's, did he?"

"I told him," she said. She started to cry again and put her hands to her face. *She told him?* I saw there were welts on the backs of her arms. My breath caught in my throat. I'd heard her mother used to carry around bruises like that.

"But why, Hannah? Why would you do that?"

"I didn't mean to. He told me to stay away from you. He said you weren't our kind and that you worked in a whorehouse. I got smart with him and said he must know all about that because I saw him in there. He started hitting me, Sonny. Hitting me and hitting me." She was crying harder. "He said he'd take a whip to you if he found you."

"But you didn't see him there. We were alone. You know that."

Her shoulders heaved as she tried to breathe. "I know. I was so angry I was just lashing out at him. I'm sorry. I'm so sorry."

I moved up closer to the porch, trying to be invisible from the street. "It's all right, Hannah. It's all right. I'll just go." She was crying too hard to answer me, so I said, "Maybe he'll cool down."

I tried to be calm for her, but I felt trapped. She looked up at me. Her face was wet from her tears. "No. He won't. He won't cool down."

"Hannah, it'll be okay. I'll stay away from you for good now."

Something else came into her eyes then. "I wanted to get inside that place, Sonny, inside Miss Lil's. I wanted to pretend I caught him in there, to know what it looked like so I could make him believe me. Momma knew about him going in there. I heard them arguing about his whoring and gambling. He used to beat her too, Sonny. Oh, how he beat her. I'm sure that's why she left me. 'Cause she feared him so."

She looked at me again. "I'm so sorry, Sonny, but I had to get in there. I needed to know. I hate him. I just hate him."

10

I went back out of town the way I came in. By the time I'd made it over the train trestle, I was pretty nearly spent from running. I put my hands on my knees and tried to catch my breath. I hopped down off the rail bed and crouched in the sand under a bare-limbed oak. I needed to think about what to do before I made things worse.

I was a mess. Hannah didn't care a whit about me. All that stuff on July Fourth and on the beach after didn't mean anything to her. She was only using me to get into Miss Lil's. I felt like a fool, of course. And it hurt a lot. I wanted so badly for her to like me, to have feelings for me like I did for her, but I think all along I'd known it was too good to be true. Like her father said, I wasn't her kind. Or at least that's what I told myself.

Now he was out there looking to kill me, and I was angry at her for getting me into this mess just so she could get back at him. But I saw the welts on her arms, and I watched her cry. I heard her say she hated him, and I knew how all of that felt too. So I was mad and hurt, feeling torn up inside. But I couldn't stay angry at her. In spite of what she'd done, I still wanted to help her. But first I had to help myself.

I was certain Mr. Dodson would go looking for me at Miss Lil's, so there was no point in going back there. If he did show up looking for me there, I knew Miss Lil would send him packing. But I wasn't so anxious to see her yet either, not if Mr. Dodson told her what I did. I couldn't stay out in the marsh all day either. I needed to be doing something. I stewed on it a while and then decided to go over to the Ocean House like Jimmy said he wanted me to. Maybe if I told the marshal that Jimmy was coming to see him, he'd be willing to help me figure how to handle Mr. Dodson. And it would give me something to keep my mind off him.

I stood up again and headed across the dunes toward the beach. I needed to stay clear of Mr. Dodson, of course, but I didn't think he'd look for me down at the marshal's hotel. The type who stayed there didn't include colored or Indians. I came out of the woods across from the Lifesaving Station and kicked the sand from my shoes. I brushed at my pants, tucked in my shirt and smoothed my hair. I made a show of staring out at the bay while I walked. I tried to look like I didn't have a care in the world so as not to attract attention, but I watched out for Mr. Dodson, skittish as a cat eyeing a dog.

The Ocean House Hotel sat where the beach road ran into South Street. The Breakwater House, where Jimmy said he was staying, was several buildings further along a crushed shell road that ran behind the hotels. The Breakwater was the finer of the two. A higher class of people stayed there in summer. The Ocean House where the marshal was staying was for the regular tourists. It was big as a barn and shaped like a box, with four stories and two chimneys and a screened-in porch that wrapped around the ground floor. Standing out in the road too long gave me the jitters, so I went around to the bayside of the building and stepped up onto the porch. The hotel's back door stood open, so I pushed aside the mosquito screen and went in.

An older girl just inside the doorway stared out at the bay. She was older than Hannah, maybe eighteen. When I came inside, the way she looked at me made me jumpy. It sounds crazy now. But with what had happened, I thought maybe Mr. Dodson had told her to watch out for me.

"Nice afternoon," she said and smiled.

Her tone was pleasant enough. Maybe she worked there and was idling. The hotel didn't look too busy. She didn't seem to notice that I and my clothes weren't fit to come in there.

"Yeah," I said, though I didn't think there was much nice about it.

"I love springtime." She gave me another kind of look. "I'm glad to be out of those winter clothes." She must have been cool enough in her flimsy cotton dress. She was just making conversation, hoping I'd visit with her and her clothes a bit. At first, I thought she was one of the upstairs girls, but she didn't seem the type. She was probably a bored towner's daughter. I guess she thought I was older than I was. With everything else going on, that wasn't something I cared about.

"Do you work here?" I asked, just to say something.

"Are you making a delivery?"

It was a strange question as I wasn't carrying anything. Maybe she'd noticed my clothes after all. "No. I'm here to meet somebody. Older guy with a long mustache. Big man, wears a funny hat."

"Oh, you mean the marshal." She rolled her eyes as if she didn't believe he was one. "He came in a bit ago. He's in one of the back rooms off the lobby." She pointed that way but frowned. "I'd tend to my business and get out if I were you. You won't be welcome in there."

"Thanks." I said. "It's a good thing you're not me, I guess."

She moved aside to let me pass and then she smiled again. "Come back by when you're done."

I didn't say yes or no to that. I didn't have time for her silliness. But her smile got bigger as if I said I would. I went through the lobby and got a nasty look from one of the guests. But with what had come my way that day, somebody staring wasn't going to bother me. I guess the manager wasn't around, though, because nobody stopped me.

I found the marshal in a back room playing cards with three other men. He'd taken off his coat and hat. His coat was folded over the back of his chair, and he'd pulled his tie loose. The room smelled like the burnt cigars and stale beer that littered on the table. The only sound was poker chips clacking, and he turned around when he heard me come in.

"Get your chores done, Mr. Sockum?"

"I'm here." I said. I wasn't there to chit-chat.

"So you are."

He clicked through a stack of chips and turned his cards face down. "Fold." He pushed the chips to the center of the table. "I'm out." The dealer shrugged. A man who'd been leaning against the wall came over to take the marshal's place at the table.

The marshal crushed his cigar into an ashtray, stood, lifted his coat and hat, and motioned to the door I'd come in. "Let's go." He didn't say anything else until we passed back through the lobby and out onto the porch. He waved at a chair. "Sit down."

I'm certain the hotel didn't want Indians using their furniture. But there was nobody else out there, so I sat. A breeze was blowing off the bay and in through the screens. It felt good. He slid another chair over so he could face me. He hung his coat and hat over the back and then sat down.

"Where's James Ryan?"

I shrugged and didn't answer him. He leaned back in the chair and tugged a fresh cigar out of his vest pocket. He bit off the tip and flicked a speck of tobacco from his mustache. Then he dug a match from another pocket and lit up. He took several puffs and watched the smoke drift up from the tip.

"He's going by the name of just Jimmy now." He saw I was going to argue, and he pointed the cigar at me. "Don't waste my time, son."

His manner was irritating, and I wasn't in the mood. "I know a man by that name. What about it?"

"You know anything about him?"

"I know his right name, so that's more than you do."

"I doubt that. What else did he tell you?"

"He said to say he's coming to see you and set you straight."

"Set me straight. About what?"

"About how you're treating me, he said, or whatever business you have with him."

The marshal chuffed—what I guess was a laugh. "Where's he want to meet?"

"How about the Breakwater House? In the gaming room tomorrow night?" Jimmy never said where or when, so I made something up.

"Tomorrow?"

"Yes. That's the message." I slid forward in the chair, getting ready to stand up. "I've got to leave. I've got business too."

He looked at me. "You interrupted a good poker hand. You ain't going 'til I'm finished with you."

I didn't sit back, but I didn't stand either.

"I'm not waiting until tomorrow night," he said. "Why don't we go back to that house of yours and get him?"

"Because he isn't there." In truth, I didn't know where Jimmy was then.

"Let me show you something, son."

He twisted around to search in his coat pocket. He pulled out a folded sheet of parchment and smoothed it on the table. It was a reward poster. The picture on it was of a younger man, and he didn't have a mustache. But there was no mistaking who it was. Someone offered four thousand dollars for Jimmy, dead or alive—except the poster said he might be calling himself James Ryan and a few other names. When I looked up, the marshal was stroking his mustache and watching me.

"That's your Jimmy, ain't it?"

"Doesn't much look like him. It isn't his name either."

"Fella's got a lot of names. That's him all right."

It dawned on me then that Jimmy had Anne looking for the poster while she was at the bank, not just finding jobs for Jimmy. I shrugged again and pushed it back to him.

"I don't care about this."

"I expect you do." He drew a long puff on the cigar. "He's an outlaw, Mr. Sockum. Robbed trains and banks in Wyoming and Utah."

I stared like that was of no importance to me, but his blue eyes just stared back. I didn't know if the poster meant trouble for Anne, but it did worry me, as I was getting mixed up with him now too.

"You're pretty far from Wyoming," I said.

"I am. Took me fall and winter and most of spring to track him to here."

"Why'd you bother? If he's an outlaw, we've got our own police."

He sat back and pulled on the cigar. "You don't know what you're mixed up in here, boy. Hanging around with Ryan could land you in trouble."

"I've already got trouble." Hannah's father wanted to kill me. What else was there to know?

"Not like the trouble he could bring down."

I stood up then. "Don't bother trying to scare me, old man. I delivered the message and now I'm going."

He looked up at me, those pale blue eyes cold as a money lender's heart. "Well, I've got a message for you to take back to him. Tell Ryan—your Mr. Lowe—if he doesn't show himself by nine o'clock tonight, I'll come down to that house and get him."

"That wouldn't be smart."

He nodded. "I'll wager your madam has the police and mayor in her dress pocket, don't she? That won't stop me, though."

"You do what you want. I'm not here to carry back your messages."

He pointed his cigar up the beach. "I can watch both the ferry and the beach road from here. You tell him I know what he's up to. Nine o'clock. You understand? Your madam ain't the only one can stir up trouble."

"I'm not going out of my way for it. If I run into him, I'll tell him."

He looked at me hard and I tried to give back as good as I got. Then I turned around and walked away. I went out the bayside door without so much as nodding at the girl. I knew now I'd need Anne's help with my problem before I delivered the marshal's message. Because I didn't think she'd be listening afterward.

11

I almost made it home before Mr. Dodson found me. He was coming down the beach road from Miss Lil's and he spotted me coming up it. The horse he was riding was as black as his suit. He stood tall in the stirrups when he saw me.

"You. Don't move."

I turned and ran. I heard him slap the horse and start after me.

"Stop, boy. You hear me?"

The horse's hooves went whuff-whuff as they churned through sand. He was closing in on me. I didn't know if he had a gun but if I stayed on the road, he'd be on me in no time. I turned off the beach and slogged up toward the dunes. A lot of sand stretched between me and a row of scrub pines, and I wasn't going to make it. People walking on the beach road had stopped to watch, but none of them came over to help me.

Something hard smacked my ear and made me stagger. I dropped onto the sand like a sack of flour. I had the presence to roll onto my side and cover my face with my hands. I looked through my fingers. Dodson pulled up on the horse and jumped down from it. He waved a riding whip around like some preacher shaking a Bible.

"Bastard."

The leather tongue snapped against my neck, barely missing my face. I rolled away and tried to scramble up the dune on all fours. The next lash caught the small of my back. I dropped onto the sand and tucked my knees. Mr. Dodson's banker shoes got dusted with sand as he worked me over, but I could see my reflection rolling around in them.

"I didn't do anything."

"Don't lie to me, boy." He raised the whip again, but thought better of it and kicked my ribs instead. "She told me what you did."

Whack. The crop came down on my head and pain shot through my eyes. I rolled to get away and he kicked me in my other side and then kicked me in the back.

"Stop it."

Someone shouted at him, but I was too occupied to look.

Whack.

"Stop it."

A snick-clack sound froze the air. Anybody who's heard that sound never forgets it—someone hand-pumping a 12-gauge shotgun. Mr. Dodson knew the sound. He stopped beating on me and spun around. I rolled farther away and twisted my head to look. I had to blink away the blood dripping in my eyes.

"What do you want?" Dodson shouted. From his tone, you'd have thought somebody had barged into his house instead of him standing out on the beach whipping me.

"Leave him alone," a familiar voice said.

The sun was in my face, so I spread my hand to shade it. Anne was like a tiger ready to pounce from Miss Lil's carriage. She had on a wide grey skirt and broad hat, and a shotgun propped across her knees. It wasn't aimed at Mr. Dodson yet, but it wasn't far off either. She looked unruffled, as if she regularly went out riding with a 12-gauge.

"This isn't your business, whore." Mr. Dodson started for her.

She lifted the shotgun. "I'll shoot you where you stand," she said. She pointed the barrel at his stomach. He stopped moving then, but he looked around as if to see if anyone was watching. He was probably embarrassed at being called down by a woman.

"I've got dealings with him. It's none of your affair."

"It is now." I was surprised at how steady her voice was. "He didn't take your daughter in there," Anne said. "Not into Miss Lil's."

He looked around again, acting nervous this time. People watching from the beach road could hear her.

I pushed myself onto my elbow.

"Are you calling my daughter a liar?" He worked hard to stand still. I could see he wanted to go at her.

"I don't know about your daughter," she said. "But when she caught you with Emily, Sonny wasn't there."

Mr. Dobson's face turned a plum color. "You're lying, wench." His voice grated loud and nasty, as if now he didn't care if someone was listening. "This god-damn Indian took my daughter in there." He slashed at my face with the crop handle, but I put my arm up in time to block it.

"Stop it." Anne waved the shotgun. "I don't know why your daughter was there that night. Maybe she came looking for you. But Sonny was with me that night. I took him into town for a soda."

I looked at her. What was she saying? Anne wasn't even home, and it was a Friday night. I don't think the drugstore was open. She was staring Mr. Dodson down, though.

"You're a god-damn liar, whore," he shouted. He brought the whip around as if he meant to use it on her. But he didn't move closer.

"Calling me names doesn't change things, Dodson." Miss Lil could let her go for talking disrespectfully to a client. She must have been sure of what she was doing. "Emily told us about your daughter seeing you there. She told all of us."

Mr. Dodson's face went blotchy. He understood Anne's threat. If he didn't back off, Miss Lil would go straight to the mayor with the story—and who knew who else? He dropped the whip to his side. "So all of you are on the negro boy's side. You don't care about what he did to my daughter."

"Watching her father's butt bounce probably left her in a state," Anne said. "No wonder she's making up stories."

Mr. Dodson looked down at me. His hand clutched the handle of the crop. "This isn't the last of it."

"Get out of here," Anne said.

He looked up and his eyes got a little wild. "You won't get away with this." He might have meant me or her, or maybe all of us. His anger burned like a wildfire. "Tell your friend…" He trailed off.

Anne wasn't having any of it. "It's over. Do you understand?"

He raised the whip again and bunched his other hand into a fist. "Who do you think you are?" He took a step toward her and she lifted the shotgun. I think she would have shot him. He did too. "You can't watch your back forever, whore, or his either. This'll come back on you. I swear it."

He turned away and walked stiff-legged to his horse. He hitched up, kicked hard at the animal's flanks and charged off toward town. He didn't look back. Anne watched him until he was out of sight.

She put the shotgun in the back of the carriage and scrambled down. I tried to stand up, but I crumpled in pain. My face and back burned with welts. I hoped my ribs weren't broken. She knelt in the sand beside me. She ran her fingers gently over my cuts. She ripped a patch from her hem and wrapped it around her hand so she could dab my face. It came away soaked with blood.

"We need to get you home." She went around behind me and put her hands under my arms. "Can you stand?"

I tried again and this time I made it. I had to lean on her to get to the carriage.

"What are you doing here? How did you find me?"

"Dodson came by the house raving about his daughter. He said he'd burn us to the ground if you didn't come out."

She helped me up onto the seat, trying not to touch my cuts as she did. I was all caked in sand and blood.

"Miss Lil got the shotgun and warned him off. She told me to come find you."

That meant Miss Lil knew. "What were you telling him about me being with you?"

She clucked at the horse and turned us around. "I told him that to get him to stop."

"But it's not true. I wasn't with you."

"It's true as it needs to be."

"Anne, I went by to see Hannah today. She told her father I took her into Miss Lil's. He beat her for it."

She looked at me a second. "Then it's your word against hers, I guess."

"No. I can't let her take the blame for it."

"Take the blame? You said she begged you to take her in, didn't you?"

"Yes."

"Then she's already to blame."

"But what's this thing about Hannah catching her father with Emily? I told you no one was in there."

She snapped the reins. "My God, Sonny. It's time you grew up."

12

When we came in the back door, Margaret saw me and moaned. She wiped her hands on her apron and came over to help Anne get me inside.

"Oh, Lord, Master Sonny. You're a terrible sight."

Anne tossed her hat on the table. Her blouse and skirt were streaked with my blood. Miss Lil was in the dining room with the other three girls. She came out to the kitchen when she saw me.

"Oh dear. He found you." She put her arm under my shoulder and helped Anne and Margaret hold me up. She was dressed for the evening and I smudged her makeup when I stumbled into her.

"Sorry, ma'am. And I'm sorry but I messed up your carriage."

"Hush. Here, let's get him onto his cot."

By then the other girls were out there hovering. I was embarrassed by all the fussing, but I was pretty lightheaded, so I didn't argue. The six of them shuffled me into the far corner of the back room that was mine. I flopped onto my cot, not caring if I bloodied the blanket. Miss Lil and Anne held my head and shoulders while Emily and Carol lifted my legs up so I could lie flat. Margaret watched—there wasn't room for another person to hold onto me. Jane just fluttered around looking helpless.

"Let's get the blood off him so we can see how badly he's hurt." Miss Lil looked at Jane, who looked back. "Get some clean towels and a basin of water." Jane looked like she didn't know where to begin, so Margaret took over.

"I'll do it," Margaret said. She was gone before Jane figured it out.

"Get these clothes off." Miss Lil nodded at my shirt. Jane seemed a little dazed, but she nodded and reached down to tug at my pants. When her hand touched blood, she pulled away and stared at it.

Miss Lil shook her head. "We need to get him unbuttoned first. Jane, get him a clean blanket."

Jane looked like she didn't want that job either, but off she went. Anne pulled off my shirt while Miss Lil worked on the buttons to my pants. Blood had spattered her fancy dress by then. I was sorry she'd need to change before her guests arrived, but she paid no heed to it. She and Anne had to work to get me out of my clothes, all caked with blood and ground-in sand. Emily tried to pull off my boot, but my foot must have swollen up. She had to struggle to do it.

Even with my pain, I was unsettled about having them undress me. I knew the girls saw men's private parts every day, but I'd never been undressed around one. Now I had four of them poking around me. I focused on Emily and Carol to keep my mind off it. I took comfort knowing they'd rather see each other's privates than gawk at mine. The two of them were kneeling on either side of me, pulling down my pants, and their hair got tangled up a little when they leaned their heads together. Emily's was thick as hemp and dark as a coal chute, while Carol's was the color of buttermilk. When they finished, I was in only my undershorts. I pulled the bedsheet over me.

Margaret came back with water and towels and Jane was right behind her carrying a folded blanket. Jane was a little older than Hannah, I think. Miss Lil dipped a cloth in the basin and wiped my face. It felt as good as a bath. I was grateful Margaret had thought to warm the water.

"Henry Dodson did this?" she asked Anne.

Anne nodded and Miss Lil made a face. "The man has a mean streak. I've seen it in town, not just today. I've spoken to John Sippel, but he won't do anything about it."

Miss Lil didn't ask why he went after me. She didn't even give me a look. I guess she knew, though, and that would come later.

Carol frowned too. "He slapped me once," she said to me. She put my trousers over by the tub next to the rest of my soiled clothes. "I grabbed his hand and screamed. Miss Lil came up and told him to leave. She said if he tried that again, he couldn't come back."

Emily looked away and reddened. I guess Dodson had been rough with her more than once, but she hadn't said anything.

Miss Lil shook her head like she didn't understand the man's behavior. "John said Dodson attends church regularly, as if that proves the man's saintly. Never mind that he drinks too much and gambles away his money, just so long as he shows up on Sunday."

I had never heard Miss Lil speak badly of a client. She must really have been put out with him.

Anne toweled off my arms. "He caught Sonny coming up the beach road. I think he'd have whipped him to death if I hadn't got there in time."

"Well, that's the last time he'll ill-treat one of my people. Since his boss won't do anything, I'll speak to Mayor Thompson tomorrow. Someone must call a halt to the man's behavior."

"I don't think he'll raise any more fuss," Anne said. "I told him we'd let it be known around if he came near Sonny again."

Miss Lil raised her eyebrows. Even though she'd just berated the man, one of her girls threatening a client didn't sit well with her.

"Why would that make any difference?" she asked her. "If he's got it in for Sonny, threats won't stop him." She looked at me. "He said you brought his daughter in here?"

So there it was, though she hadn't asked me if it was true. I looked at her a bit, working up my courage to tell her.

"That's what his daughter told him," Anne said, "but it's not true."

I was surprised. Why would Anne lie to Miss Lil about that? Jane stared at me. Maybe she didn't think I had it in me.

"No?" Miss Lil still looked at me, waiting for me to agree.

Anne said, "Sonny was with me when it happened. We went for a walk on the beach that night."

In this version we weren't having a soda. She must have caught her mistake about the drugstore.

"A walk?"

"You saw how wrought up Sonny was today, Lil. That girl has been vexing him for weeks. He told me all about it while we walked. We got back sometime after nine."

Miss Lil looked at me and I nodded, trying to look upset about Hannah. It wasn't hard. She frowned at Anne. "Why would his daughter make up such a story?"

"Because she was in here. She caught her father with Emily."

I didn't know what to say about that.

Miss Lil put down the washcloth and glared at the girls, first at Emily and then at the other two. "So there was a young girl in this house. Who allowed that?" She looked like she might whip somebody too.

"No one did, Lil," Anne said. "It was still early on a Friday night. The rest of us were off, even Margaret. Dodson had a session with Emily, though. His daughter must have followed him here and come in looking for him."

"Dodson was here with you?" Miss Lil was talking to Emily.

She nodded. "Yes, ma'am. You know how he likes to come around when there's little chance of him being seen. He'd arranged it for that evening."

"On a Friday," Anne said again.

"Yes. Early on a Friday," Emily repeated. "He knew no one would be about."

"It wasn't written down. Who recorded it?"

"I did, ma'am, since I was the only one here. I must have got the day mixed up, though. I'm not good at those things."

Miss Lil considered that. "Where was she when she saw you?"

Friday night? Did Hannah come back here again that night after I showed her around? I looked over at Anne. She nodded.

Emily looked at the floor. Her face turned pink as a trout. "In the hallway outside my room, ma'am."

"You were in the hallway?"

"No ma'am. His daughter was. He was in my room."

"Were you servicing him?"

Emily nodded. "He was naked as a jay. He must have heard something 'cause he looked around. I saw the girl standing out there, but she took off before he saw her good. He asked me about it, but I said it was just one of the girls come back. I didn't know it was his daughter. I didn't know who it was then. He couldn't go running after her, though, naked like he was, and neither could I."

"Had he been drinking?"

Emily looked down. "You don't allow that in the rooms, Miss Lil."

That meant he had. Miss Lil's frown got deeper, but then she let that go by. She sat down on the edge of my cot but kept looking at Emily. "Oh, my Lord. The poor thing. What were you thinking, leaving your door open?"

"It was unseasonal hot that evening, ma'am. You know how those rooms get. I didn't think no one else would be here."

Miss Lil shook her head. "Why didn't you say something?"

Emily looked away. "I don't know, ma'am. I was afraid you'd be mad."

Miss Lil looked afflicted. "I still don't understand why she'd come in here." She looked at me again. Her eyes were black as her dress. "Weren't you and Anne talking about her this morning, how she was giving you fits?"

"Yes, ma'am," I said. I knew what was coming next.

"Did she come in here looking for you?"

I must have paused a second or two, but it seemed a lot longer. "I guess she could have, ma'am. I don't know. I wasn't here then."

"Does she know what kind of work we do here?"

"Yes, ma'am."

"But you didn't bring her in here?"

Miss Lil stared hard at me. I glanced at Anne and she shook her head a little. They waited for me to answer. Whatever I said next, I knew I wasn't going to feel good about it. The girls and Margaret all kept still. None of them wanted to be shushed out of the room just then.

"No, ma'am. She's headstrong, Miss Lil. If she was in here that night, she came in on her own." It wasn't exactly a lie, but it prayed in the same church.

I'd done it. I'd jumped off the bridge into the marsh. Anne relaxed and Miss Lil looked away. Just giving her my word had satisfied her. She looked at Anne again. "That was weeks ago. Why is he bringing it up now?"

"I don't know," Anne said. "Maybe he got nasty with his daughter and she blurted out that she'd seen him here."

"And she blamed Sonny for bringing her here?"

"Probably to soften it for herself."

"That might be, Anne, but Dodson thinks it's true. Make no mistake. He can make trouble for us. And if word gets out that his daughter was in here, the mayor won't raise a hand to help us."

"But Dodson was in here that night. We have that over him, don't we?"

"Do we?" Miss Lil didn't look persuaded. "I hope you're right about him. Maybe when he cools down, he'll see that if he raises a fuss, it could come back on him." She winced as if to say she didn't have a better plan. "I'll need to say something to the mayor, though. Quietly—to protect us."

"You going to tell him that Dodson comes here?"

"He knows that. I'm going to tell him that he slapped one of my girls. Somebody's bound to say they saw Dodson whipping up on Sonny today. The mayor will want to know about it. I'll make up something he'll believe. I'll keep it as close to the truth as I can just in case Dodson starts raising a fuss."

She dipped the cloth into the basin and used it to dab blood from my chest. She asked Anne, "If you weren't here that night, how did you know what happened?"

It was a good question. I'd just told Anne about me and Hannah that morning and she'd made up her story about Mr. Dodson on the spot.

"I told her," Emily said, "right after she came back that night. I didn't know who else to tell."

"Except me?" Miss Lil gave her a look that could sour cream.

Emily lowered her eyes again. "Yes, ma'am. I'm sorry. I knew you wouldn't be happy about it. Anne's the one told me she thought it might be Mr. Dodson's daughter."

Anne nodded. "I guess I had her on my mind, what with Sonny and me just coming back from talking about her."

"Well, I'm not happy, Emily. Something like this affects all of us. You should have told me right after it happened."

"Yes, ma'am."

"You too, Anne."

Anne nodded.

"It doesn't matter who it was. A young girl came into this house. That's serious. Do you understand that?"

"Yes, ma'am."

Miss Lil shook her head in that way she had. "We'll talk some more about this later, Emily."

She finished dabbing off my chest. She put the bloodied cloth in the basin and wiped me down with a dry towel.

"That's as much as we're going to get off."

She wrapped some cotton bandages over the cuts on my neck and arms where the whip had broken the skin. She felt around my head for bumps and ran her fingers across my welts. "These should heal, though they're going to look ugly for a time."

I flinched when she poked at my ribs.

"How does that feel?"

"It hurts a bit, ma'am." It hurt more than a bit.

"I don't think there's anything broken, but we'll wait a few days. If it's still swollen, we'll have Dr. Orr take a look."

"Yes, ma'am."

"You need to take it easy for a bit."

"Yes, ma'am. I'll be careful doing my chores."

"No more chores this week, I think."

"But, ma'am, I'm fine."

"I'll get some temporary help. Margaret filled in for you today, but she's already got too much to do."

Margaret gave her a smile. "Be glad to, Miss Lil. It won't be a problem."

"Considering that you were out doing Jimmy's bidding," Miss Lil said to me, "he should be responsible for this. I mean to ask him to pay to have someone fill in."

Anne must have told her why I'd gone out.

Margaret nodded, still smiling. "Really, Miss Lil, I could surely use the money. Things have been tight of late."

Miss Lil looked at her. She'd give in. She knew Margaret's man didn't bring in much money.

Miss Lil wiped her hands on a clean towel and dabbed water on the spots on her dress. I struggled to sit up, pretending it didn't hurt as bad as it did. She put a hand on my shoulder.

"Not too fast."

I lay back down. I could only do so much pretending at that point.

"Maybe I will rest a bit," I said. "I'll be able to get up after."

Miss Lil stood up. "All right, girls. You've lollygagged enough. Go upstairs and get ready for supper. Our first guest arrives at seven."

Carol, Emily and Jane bustled out of the room, whispering as they went up the stairs. I guess I was their entertainment that day. Margaret looked at me and made a sad face. She might be happy for the extra money, but she was worried about me too. I was grateful for that. She shook her head and went out to collect wood for the stove. Everyone was being nice to me and all because they believed my lies. I felt like I deserved that whipping.

Anne hung back, though. As Miss Lil got up, she touched her sleeve.

"Could I take part of the evening off, Miss Lil?"

Miss Lil frowned. "I have a business to run." Before Anne could argue, she added, "Jimmy pays me well enough for your time, Anne, but I have other clients to think of too. Men don't like to wait long for their turn."

"Yes, ma'am. Maybe just an hour or so then this afternoon? I need to find Jimmy and tell him what Sonny found out from that marshal." Anne looked at me, wanting to know what that was.

Miss Lil asked me for her. "Did you see him?"

"Yes, ma'am, I did. He wants to meet with Jimmy tonight."

Anne looked anxious.

Miss Lil looked at her. "I'm not happy about Jimmy bringing his trouble in here, Anne."

Anne didn't say anything to that, but I could see she fretted more about Jimmy than Miss Lil right then.

"Be back by six. No later."

Anne's smile showed her relief. "I promise I will."

Miss Lil didn't smile back. "I mean it, Anne. Six. And tell Jimmy I want no part of what he's brought on himself. I run a good place. Our clients trust us. I won't condone anything that undoes that."

Anne looked at the floor. It looked like she wanted to run right out and find Jimmy, but she was waiting for Miss Lil to leave so she could talk to me. Miss Lil knew that too, but she took time to check that my bandages weren't leaking.

"Six," she told Anne a third time. It wasn't like her to repeat herself. She went out to the kitchen and left the two of us alone.

Anne crouched down beside the cot. "The marshal said tonight?"

"He said he won't wait until tomorrow. I guess he thinks Jimmy will run off."

"Jimmy said he can't do it tonight."

"Why? Because he has a faro game? I told the marshal, but it didn't matter to him."

"What's he going to do if he doesn't show up?"

"He said he'll come down here." I could see that worried her. "He showed me a wanted poster."

Anne didn't look at me, which meant she knew about it. "What of it?"

"It said that Jimmy's a robber and there's a reward for him. Dead or alive." I added that to see how she'd react to it.

She didn't say anything at first. "Posters don't make someone bad, Sonny. There's a mistake is all."

"That's why you went to the bank, isn't it? To see if his poster was hanging up there?" She must have been very worried about it. We were a long way from Wyoming.

"Jimmy's done a lot of good for folks. Someone had a grudge against him because of people he used to run around with."

She knew a lot more about it than what was on the poster.

Maybe she believed Jimmy about it being a mistake, but I didn't. "The marshal tracked him down here from out west," I said. "Are you in trouble because of him, Anne?"

"I need to find him."

She didn't answer my question and that worried me. She said it like she was hoping I would help her. I was angry at her for even thinking that, seeing what shape I was in. But I owed her for Mr. Dodson. "Maybe I can go with you." I started to get up but couldn't. I lay back again and shook my head. "I feel bad about the lies. Miss Lil deserves better from me, and you lying to Mr. Dodson about me will make it go harder on Hannah."

"Only if he believes me. Anyway, she'll get what she deserves." Her face softened a little and she put her hand on my arm. "I know this is hard on you, but I want you to trust me about something."

"What?" I was having trouble trusting her then.

"You didn't get Hannah in trouble."

I looked away. No matter what Hannah said, I don't think she'd have gone to Miss Lil's place if not for me. "I brought her in here."

"Because she wanted you to." Her eyes were hard again. "Sonny, whatever her reasons were, she did this to herself. And now by telling her father, she's put you in real danger."

I didn't like hearing that, but I knew it was true.

She brushed the hair out of my eyes. It was a little thing, but it comforted me.

"My lying for you is better than you getting killed because Hannah told the truth. She used you." There it was again. She stood. "I'm going to find Jimmy. He needs to hear what the marshal said."

"Okay."

My face hurt like the devil. I wanted to be done with Jimmy and the marshal and Hannah's father. Unlucky for me, that wasn't to be.

13

My cot was pushed into a corner between shelves so crammed with vegetable tins and canning jars that I had to keep my belongings in an old crate under my bed. We'd tucked a wicker fold-up screen in there by the clawfoot tub if need be, though Margaret made me leave the room when one of the girls was using it. We didn't have electric lights. We got our water from a well outside the kitchen door. Day or night, summer and winter, we had to traipse to the outhouse behind the stable to do our business. Some things don't change much.

By the time Anne came back, I'd slept a little. I still ached all over, but most of the bleeding had stopped and I had on clean clothes, so I felt better. Anne didn't keep her word. She was back well after six o'clock and she brought Jimmy with her too. If Miss Lil had come in then, she'd likely have turned both of them out on the spot. Jimmy had on a leather coat and he'd tied a bandana around his neck. He looked like he'd been out riding. He wasn't wearing his big-faced grin. He looked like he was anxious to know what the marshal had said, but I credit him for asking about my whipping first.

"Judas, kid. You look a sight. The girl's father did all this?"

I'd put on a clean shirt and pants, but my face and arms were a mess.

"It was awful to watch," Anne said. "Dodson had himself worked up."

"Well then, it's a good thing you came along. This seems pretty stiff fare just for mounting his daughter."

I wanted to jump up and go at him, but I didn't have it in me. I just stared and said nothing.

"He didn't touch her, Jimmy," Anne said. "Leave him be. He's been through enough."

At least Anne was showing concern. Jimmy looked surprised. I guess he didn't think he'd said anything hurtful.

"Dodson will get what's coming to him," Anne said.

Jimmy looked at her for a second, as if surprised by what she'd said. He said to me, "If there's any justice, he will."

I didn't know what to make of that, but if he meant he'd go thrash Dodson himself, I'd have done just about anything he asked me to.

"Tell Jimmy what the marshal said."

I did and he wasn't happy with what he heard.

"Why, the skunk can't even wait a day? Makes me sorry I offered to talk to him." He stroked his thin mustache with the side of his finger, just the way the marshal did, though he had less to stroke. "I guess that's what I get for being accommodating."

"He thinks you'll run off if he waits."

"Run off? Why should I run off? I'm as eager to straighten this out as the next man."

I doubted that. Anne was watching him and not saying anything.

"What about that reward poster?" I asked.

Anne glanced at the floor, but Jimmy put on a little smile. "That's not me, kid."

"Sure looks like you. You were younger, but there's no mistaking your face."

"It's my face all right, but I didn't do what it says on there. They got the wrong man."

"Must be a lot of things you didn't do, Jimmy, for them to write all that."

"It's a big mistake is all. I got mixed up with a bunch a few years back that had too much time on their hands. We'd get drunk and such, maybe raise some Cain, but I came to my senses and we parted ways. It was after I broke off with them that they robbed a bank."

"Several banks according the poster. And trains."

"I wasn't a part of any of it, kid. But since I'd been seen in their company, I got accused of it."

"That bunch did all this and the only picture they got is yours?"

"I'm the only one ever had his picture took."

Jimmy had a way about him. From his face you could almost believe he was telling the truth.

"So you're not this James Ryan the marshal's looking for?"

"No. That was a mix-up too. Ryan ran with them, probably helped with the robbery. I don't know. But my picture went out with his name."

That was too much. "So the marshal's looking for the wrong man with the wrong name? Why don't you go explain it all to him?"

"I will, kid. That's what I said. But I can't go tonight. I got too much going on." I wondered what he was up to, but if I asked him, he'd tell me another story. He looked at Anne. "You got any ideas?"

She looked worried enough for both of them. "I'll go see him after I get off work. It'll be later than he wants, but I guess he'll have to wait a bit."

Jimmy looked like he was considering letting her do that.

"He told me by nine," I said, "and he seemed set on it. Anyway, I thought you were going to play faro at the Ocean House. That's where he's staying."

"I'm not playing cards tonight. I got other things need tending to." He looked at Anne. "Why can't you go now, before your man—what's his name, Sweetland, comes by?"

I was surprised. Miss Lil didn't let the girls talk about the guests or when they came and went. Anne shot a glance at me. She knew better too. What else had she shared with him?

"I can't. I promised Miss Lil I'd work this evening."

"Work? I'm paying her more than she'll get from you working."

"That's not it, Jimmy. I promised her."

"And what about Sweetland? That ain't work enough?"

"Lil needs me to help with the early trade. I'll go on down there after. It won't be real late I don't think."

"You need to go now, Anne. Later might not be good enough for him."

Anne was getting annoyed, but she wanted to help Jimmy too. "Maybe I can get away for a while when Sweetland's here. He won't care, I think, since he'll be here all night. He'll need a break." She realized what she'd said and gave me an embarrassed look.

"No, Anne. I need you to stay with him." Jimmy looked at me as if I'd heard something I shouldn't, which made me wonder what. Then he said, "If I don't show up on time, the marshal will come here looking for me. We can't have that. Go see him now. Please. It's important."

She looked pained. "I'm sorry, Jimmy. I just can't."

I thought he'd get angry but instead he looked like a lost hound. I was glad she'd showed him some spine. Jimmy stared at her a while, probably hoping his puppy dog look would change her mind. Then he looked at me like he'd heard what I was thinking.

"You feeling up to seeing that marshal again, kid?"

"No," I said at the same time Anne did.

"He's in no shape to be running around."

"I was just asking since you won't go."

His mooning didn't work on me either. "I told you. I'm not running any more errands for you."

"That was before Dodson whipped up on you, kid. But since Anne helped you out there, I'd think you'd be grateful enough to help her out now."

"You didn't have anything to do with that. And besides, it's your errand, not hers."

"But she's the one who can't go."

"He can't be going out." Anne was really worried about me,

which made me feel guilty, because I planned to go out as soon as they left.

"He could reopen those cuts. Besides, he might have broken something."

"He don't look like nothin's broken."

He was right. I'd been beat on harder than that and came through it just fine. "I'm not going," I said.

Jimmy looked a little unsettled, which was unusual in him. Whatever he was up to, it was plain he didn't want the marshal interfering. He gave Anne a look like he was hoping she'd talk me into it. She didn't try, which made me feel both better and worse.

I wanted to see Hannah to find out if her father had hurt her again. I wasn't sure how to do it at this late hour, but I was determined to go. In spite of what she'd told him, I was still worried about her.

"Come on, kid. Just one more time?"

Because Jimmy was bent on asking me questions, I had one for him. "What kind of work is my brother doing for you?" I was taking a shot in the dark and must have hit the target.

The side of his mouth turned up like he had no idea what I was talking about. "I don't know your brother, do I?"

Anne first looked at me and then at Jimmy. "What's Daniel got to do with this?" She'd seen him when he came by to talk to me from time to time.

"Daniel?" His eyebrows went up. "Big strappin' boy? Long hair like yours? That's your brother? Now that I think about it, you do favor him."

I wasn't sure if he didn't know or was just acting.

"He told me he was working for you," I said, though that wasn't what Daniel said. "What's he mixed up in?"

"Mixed up in? Why, nothing. Just does a few odd jobs is all. Why? What did he tell you?"

"He said I should ask you about it."

Jimmy grinned. "It's nothing to worry about, kid. I can't move about town with the chance one of those posters might turn up, can I? So I just had him do some errands for me."

"My brother's decent, but he can be a bad sort if he gets with the wrong lot."

"I'm sure you're right, kid."

"Sort of like you, Jimmy." I could feel my blood rise. "He's my only family. I don't want him tangled up with you."

"He's fine."

"Then what's he doing?"

"Just errands. Hires me a horse when I need one. Brings me supplies when I can't get into town. It's honest labor and I pay him for it."

"He said it was secret. What's secret about that?"

Anne looked at Jimmy like she had the same question.

"I told him not to say he was working for me is all. I don't need to call notice to myself." He used his moon-faced grin again. "In fact, that gives me an idea. I'll see if I can find him and have him go see the marshal."

A pain shot up my side as I stood so I could look him in the eye. "Leave him out of this. I don't want him in trouble."

"What's trouble about that? The marshal didn't give you trouble, did he? Only trouble you found was on the way back here."

"I don't believe you, Jimmy. I think you're up to no good."

He spread out his arms like maybe I'd crucified him. "Come on, kid, what do you take me for? I have enough problems dogging me already. You think I want to get mixed up with something here?" I didn't answer, so he put his hands on my shoulders. I winced. "Don't worry about your brother. You should be glad he's got a job."

I shrugged off his hands and stepped away from him. "You don't know anything about him." He was right, though. I was surprised to see Daniel sober when I met him on the trestle bridge.

He put his hands down. "You're right. I don't. I'm sorry I said that."

"Just leave Daniel out of it."

He smiled. "Well, let's make it a fair trade. How 'bout I pay you to go instead?" He pulled a dollar treasury note from his coat and pressed it into my hand. I folded it in half and put it in my pants pocket.

Jimmy smiled. "I appreciate that, kid. I really do."

I had a feeling I'd just agreed to what he knew all along I'd do. I stooped over to get my coat from under my cot, but my back was so tender I had to kneel for it instead.

Anne touched my arm. "You don't need to do this. What if you run into Dodson?"

I stood up and Anne took away her hand. "It's late enough that he's probably at home. I'll be fine." If he wasn't, I'd really have to be careful. I didn't have a plan.

"I'll bet you will." Jimmy nodded. "What are you going to tell him? The marshal, I mean."

"I don't know. I'll decide when I see him."

"Try to get him to give me 'til tomorrow morning at least. Don't work him up into coming back here."

"Okay."

"Be careful, Sonny," Anne said.

"I will." I left them there, went through the kitchen and out the back door. I had no intention of calling on the marshal again.

14

Once I got into town, I crept around the side of Hannah's house, squatted down under the window and peeked in. Hannah and her father were arguing. Both were shouting at the same time, and I didn't need to hear all the words to know what it was about. Dodson waved his arms around and his face was red from yelling. She was crying but standing up to him. It didn't look like he'd hit her again. Maybe he feared what people would say when they saw her, especially once word got around about how he took after me. Whipping an Indian for being around his daughter was one thing, I guess, but thrashing her probably wouldn't go well down at his church, not after all the whispering about what he'd done to his wife.

I don't know what I expected to do by going over there. Maybe she'd come running out and I could stand up to her father the way Daniel stood up against Pa, though I hadn't considered how I might do that. I thought about Anne taking him on to defend me, but she had the shotgun and I only had me. Watching them go at it threw water on that idea anyway. She held her own with him and never looked my way. She did a darned sight better against him than I had over on the beach. I stayed there and listened until they finally quieted down. He said something hard and she snapped something back at him and then her small feet ran up the stairs. A door slammed—probably hers—and after a few minutes more he went out the front door and slammed it behind him. I hunkered down but he never looked my way. He went stomping off stiff-legged toward town.

I left and walked along the edges of the town, thinking about Hannah and then about Daniel, wondering what I should do about either one of them. I felt bad too for not going to see the marshal like Anne thought I would, but I didn't have the stomach for talking to him just then. So I wandered down by the beach until after seven, holding off going home so I wouldn't run into Anne or Jimmy.

When I got back near our pier, the Army gunboat had tied up. The Corps of Engineers sent it down river from Philadelphia every month during the summer carrying the payroll for the breakwater contractors. Lots of company boats ran out to the new breakwater every day, and maybe a hundred or more hired laborers worked on it—at least to judge from the shantytown that sprung up on the beach each spring. The Army didn't seem to like to have that much money moving around. A dozen or so soldiers guarded that boat.

Seeing the boat docked ticked in my mind. Something there should ring a bell, something about the Army man in charge. I remembered he made a habit of visiting Miss Lil's whenever his boat was in town. It took me a minute to remember his name, but when I did the pieces started to fall into place. Sweetland. Captain Sweetland. He was the one spending that very night with Anne. And Jimmy had jumped at her when she said she'd slip out while Sweetland was in there to go see the marshal. Why was Jimmy interested in Sweetland? I thought about that poster the marshal had showed me and my heart stopped. The payroll. It dawned on me that Jimmy probably planned to get his hands on it. In fact, I was suddenly certain of it.

And Daniel worked for him.

I needed to tell somebody, to find some way to stop him. I rushed back to Miss Lil's looking for Anne, but she was upstairs. Miss Lil was greeting guests in the parlor and didn't have time for me. My only other choice was to try to find Jimmy myself. I didn't care about his trouble with the law, or even whether he was going to steal the Army's payroll. My worry now was Daniel. If he was mixed up in it and they caught him, he'd be the first one they'd throw in jail. And I didn't have much time. The city police would move the payroll from the Army boat to the bank first thing in the morning.

That's why Jimmy wanted to put off meeting the marshal. He planned to be long gone by tomorrow night. The marshal coming for him must have put a knot in his plans. Knowing Jimmy, he'd find a way to untie it.

The problem was, where was he hiding? Not in Anne's room. Sweetland was probably there or soon would be. I thought about the stable and went to look. The mare was in there half asleep, but no Jimmy. There wasn't any place in town he could go. It buttoned up like a shoe by that hour on a weekday night. He could have gone back to his hotel, but he knew the marshal would watch for him to show up there. He could have holed up at the Clubhouse by the pier, but usually old boozers just played penny ante poker in there. It didn't seem to suit him.

I went back inside, not sure where to turn. Maybe I could find Daniel and talk sense into him, though he didn't seem much interested in listening to me. Besides, I didn't know where he was either.

That's when it struck me where he was. I grabbed my coat and went out to saddle the mare. I knew I should ask Miss Lil first, but she was busy with the guests and I knew she'd try to talk me out of it. I led the mare out of the stable, climbed up on her back and nudged her through the gate. It was a long way to our grandmother's old cabin. That mare was fat and lazy and wouldn't go much above a trot, so it would take me a couple of hours to get out there. But I was sure now that I'd find Daniel there—and Jimmy with him. Moonlight was just bright enough to see by.

15

Our old farm was ten miles west of town and it was a real trial getting out there after dark, especially with my bruises complaining every time that careless mare stumbled. A lot of Nanticoke used to live out that way, but most of them had either drifted away or gone white. The area had gone back to weeds and new growth trees. When Ma was alive, we used to make a little money off a couple of pigs and some chickens, minus whatever Pa drank up.

When I came out of the trees the moon hadn't set, so it must have been before ten. The crickets stopped chirruping when they heard the mare and a big owl flew off, rustling the leaves behind him. I hadn't been out there since I started at Miss Lil's. But even in the half-dark, I could see Daniel had let the place go to shambles. Both front windows were broken out. Cardboard the wind had shredded covered one, and the other was empty as a lost tooth. Two horses were tied up out front. One was an old plow my brother had bought and the other one I didn't know.

Daniel must have heard me coming up because the door opened. He stood there in the center of it with a shotgun in one hand and a lamp in the other. He was shirtless and now barefoot too. He recognized me but didn't say anything, so I climbed down and tied the mare to a tree. I heard a horse chuff, not one of the ones out front, and I shaded my eyes from the lantern's light and looked where the sound came from. Three more hobbled horses grazed on the side of the house near the trees. From what I could see, they looked like fine animals. I guessed they were hired. At least I hoped so.

"What do you want?" Daniel finally asked me when I looked back. He didn't sound angry at me, just not very friendly.

"Whose horses?" I tried not to sound like I was accusing him of anything.

"Never mind about them. What are you doing out here?"

"I need to talk to you. And Jimmy."

"Jimmy's not here."

I paused a second before saying, "I think he is. That's his horse, I'd guess." I pointed to the one tied next to me.

"Why don't you go back to town, Sonny? This ain't a good time to visit."

He took a step out into the yard, put the lamp on the ground and let the shotgun droop in his arm. "You can tell me what you want tomorrow."

"I need to tell you tonight." I walked up until I was standing just in front of him. I couldn't see his eyes well enough to tell if he was drunk. "I want to come in."

He looked me over, noticing the bruises on my face, and then my arms.

"What happened? You fall off that whore's roof?"

"Where's Jimmy?"

He tensed a little. "You gave up the house when you moved to town."

I needed to figure how to go at this. We were going to have it out if I pushed him too hard. Jimmy fixed the problem for me.

"It's okay. Let him come in."

He moved into the door opening. Daniel half-glanced over his shoulder at him but didn't move out of my way. "It ain't yours to say," he said to Jimmy.

Jimmy acted as if he hadn't heard him. "Hello, kid. Must be

important for you to come out this late." He was something. He didn't even act surprised I knew where he was.

"I thought I'd find you here." I started to go around Daniel, but he moved to block me. "Daniel, I need to talk. It's important."

"Say what you need to out here."

I looked away and made myself take a breath. He had no business keeping me out. I was tempted to push him aside. But that would cause a fight and that's not why I was out there.

"I can't. There's some things you need to hear about. Both of you."

"We need to get inside, kid. There's no telling who'll come riding up next."

Daniel frowned. I thought he'd go off on Jimmy, but he surprised me.

"Just for a bit then."

He leaned over to get the lamp and I stepped around him. He followed me inside and then leaned the shotgun against the wall behind the door.

I saw why he didn't want me in there. He was probably ashamed. Our kitchen and eating space was a ruin. Whiskey bottles—empties—were scattered around like cobs for the pig. It was cheap stuff. I don't know what he ate, but a rusted-out tub in the corner overflowed with dishes streaked in dried-on filth. Whatever he'd left on them had turned nasty, and a sickly stench hung over the room. He'd started another stack on the floor. I wondered where he got so many of them. They looked like plates the hotels use.

He hadn't cleaned up in months or maybe ever. Dry mud clods littered the floor, along with enough scattered old straw to feed the horse. He'd tossed a flea-infested mattress on the floor. Feathers stuck out of the split tacking like darts. The rest of the room furniture was a beat-up wood table and one chair. The table was nailed together from rough cut wood and the legs weren't even. Our old wood stove still stood in the corner but its chimney was gone. It vented right into the room. It's a wonder he hadn't burned the place down. I was mad enough to spit at him, but I didn't.

Daniel read my look and glared. He didn't take well to being criticized, even if nothing was said.

"Okay, you're here. Say your piece and get going."

He wasn't drunk, though his eyes were bloodshot. It wasn't from drinking too much alcohol then, but from needing it so bad. Jimmy must have paid him pretty well for him to work that hard at staying sober.

I looked at Jimmy. "You're planning to steal the Army payroll, aren't you?"

Jimmy acted so surprised his head actually jerked back. He recovered from his shock and put on a wide-eyed grin. I noticed Daniel hadn't seemed surprised by my question.

"The Army payroll? I don't know what you're talking about. The marshal put you up to asking me that?"

Daniel leaned in so close I could smell stale liquor on his breath. I guess it hadn't been as long as I thought. "What's he talking about? What marshal?"

I kept looking to Jimmy, hoping to keep Daniel at bay a little. "Nobody told me anything, I figured it out. You plotting with Anne to keep Colonel Sweetland occupied all night. You've brewed up some plan to take that money while he's at Miss Lil's, haven't you?"

Jimmy shook his head and smiled. "So you think Anne keeping company gets the Army's money robbed? Kid, you've got some imagination. You sure the marshal didn't put this in your head?"

Saying it out loud, it did sound far-fetched. But from the way he'd talked to Anne about Sweetland and watching Daniel now, I was certain I was onto something.

"I don't care what you've got planned. Just keep Daniel out of it."

Daniel gave me an ill-tempered look. "I ain't the one you need to worry about. This isn't your business."

That didn't sound good. I looked at Jimmy. He pretended to be bewildered by what Daniel might have meant.

"Jimmy, either promise me you won't get Daniel involved, or so help me, I'll go tell the marshal what I know. I suspect he won't think it's funny."

Daniel stepped in closer and raised a fist. "You've been talking to a marshal? What the hell do you think you're doing?"

Jimmy stretched his arm between us. He pulled on my shoulder to move me away from my brother. I winced but didn't let him see it.

"What did he do, kid? Make you his deputy?"

Daniel was seething. "You better damn worry about yourself, Sonny. I don't need your help."

Jimmy put his other hand flat on Daniel's chest. I guess it was his way of trying to take us down a bit. It didn't work on me, and it wasn't working on Daniel. He looked at Daniel and said to me, "I think your brother's old enough to look out for himself."

Daniel calmed down a little at that. I didn't.

"I mean it, Jimmy. I'm tired of your lying. I didn't go see the marshal."

Jimmy lowered his arms and looked at me. "You're a fine one to talk about lying. You said you'd see the marshal for me, and you didn't. Hell, late as it is, he probably already went to Lil's and made a fuss. I'll bet she and Anne are mighty upset right now you didn't keep your word."

I didn't say anything. I'd forgotten the marshal said he'd come looking for Jimmy if he didn't show by nine. If he did go there, though, Miss Lil could handle him. Anne was likely angry with me.

"And what am I supposed to do now? I told you I got business to finish, but because of your lying, I can't go into town without him hunting for me."

Daniel's eyes flared. "You've had your say, Sonny. Get back to your whorehouse." He wasn't sure what was going on, but he knew my being there was the problem.

Jimmy wasn't ready to let it go yet. "Robbing the payroll?" He laughed out loud then, sounding like a braying mule. "That's just crazy. Look, kid, even if someone was crazy enough to try such a thing, hell, half the U.S. Army came to town on that boat today. Or were you beyond noticing that in the fever you've got for Dodson's girl?"

"I guess I'll find out what the marshal thinks of it then." I admit it did sound crazy.

Daniel shook his head and went to window and looked out. "Come on, Jimmy. Get him out of here." He seemed nervous now, like he was worried this mysterious marshal would come riding up outside.

"Remember what that reward poster says you did?" I asked Jimmy. "I guess the marshal thinks you're crazy enough to try it."

Daniel looked back at me. "Why don't you just shut up about the damned marshal?" He wanted to ask me about the poster, but he didn't want it to look like he wasn't in on it. It seemed Jimmy hadn't told him a lot of things.

"Oh, so that's it. He just wants the reward. It don't matter to him if I'm innocent or not. He makes up some story about me robbing the payroll to get you working on his side, maybe to lead him right to me."

I shook my head. He was a master at twisting people's words. "I told you. I didn't talk to him."

I looked away. I hadn't told him it was me who made up the story about the payroll robbery.

Jimmy misread my look. "Hah. I thought so. He played you, kid." He waved at the door. "Hell, he might have followed you right out here."

Daniel came over and stood next to us. "What reward poster?" he asked.

Jimmy shrugged. "Okay. Now you've had your say. You can get out of here."

Jimmy didn't act like he was really worried about the marshal showing up, but Daniel did. He bent to look through the broken window.

"Damn you, Sonny."

I could hear the crickets going at it, so it wasn't likely anyone was out there. Daniel looked at the shotgun. "Who's out there?" He looked like he wanted to start shooting at the shadows.

"Just some old man your brother made friends with."

Daniel looked at me. "Why the hell are you doing this?"

I shook my head. "First of all, he's not my friend. Jimmy paid me to go talk to him."

Daniel frowned and looked at Jimmy. "Is he right? Why would you pay him to talk to somebody like that?"

He was getting lost in the turns of our talk. Picking up on things wasn't what he was quick at. I had to be careful not to treat him like he was slow. He'd go off if he thought I did. And besides, I owed him better, and I hoped Jimmy knew that.

When Jimmy still didn't answer him, I said, "Nobody followed me here. I'm not a halfwit."

Daniel didn't look convinced. Jimmy was grinning.

"I know he didn't follow you, kid. You're an Injun."

I wasn't as cocksure as I pretended to be. I'd doubled back a couple of times on my way out there and watched to see if anyone was coming. The marshal said he'd tracked Jimmy all the way from Wyoming, so he might be good enough to come up on us without stirring up the crickets.

I pushed on. "The marshal says he has proof." Daniel looked at me and I looked back. "I came out here to warn you. Jimmy's getting you in trouble."

"The only one's giving me trouble is you." He glanced at the door. "Maybe we should take a look around, Jimmy."

Jimmy was focused on what I'd said. "Proof. Is that right?" From his tone he let me know he didn't believe it. "He didn't say what this proof is, I suppose?"

I thought about making something up, but I was already in over my head. "He wouldn't say. I don't think he trusts me too much."

"Me and him agree on that," Daniel said.

"How convenient." Jimmy stepped back and stretched his arms as if to say he couldn't believe what he was hearing. "This is just fine. I pay you to go talk to him and you come back accusing me of being a robber. If that don't beat all."

Daniel watched us. I guess he'd decided to wait until I left to get answers from Jimmy. I wished him good luck doing that.

"I'll tell you something, kid. That marshal of yours is a

gunfighter, a killer. Him and his brothers were tried for murdering cowboys down in Arizona. He run off afterward."

"So now you know all about him? And how do you know that? Did he have a wanted poster too?" I knew I was about to hear another of his stories.

"I can read, can't I?" His tone was mocking me as if he'd pulled a fast one. "I read about him in a newspaper."

"When did you have time to read newspapers? You just today found out who he was."

He smiled like he was glad I'd asked him. "I'll tell you when. Today. When Anne told me he showed up at the house, I went to town and poked around. A fella at the newspaper office showed me a news story about him that ran some time ago."

"Our town newspaper had a story in it about the marshal? Why in the world would that be?" I shook my head at how far he'd gone with this.

"Because your marshal is famous, Sonny, people all over the country know about his gunfighting ways. His being in town has got folks here stirred up."

I could believe Jimmy had made friends down at the *Delaware Pilot.* He pointed his finger at me then as if that proved he was right.

"That's your marshal, kid. I don't suppose he told you that while he was filling your head with lies about me."

"And all you've ever done is lie, Jimmy, so that part don't make him special."

"A gunman's come here?" Daniel looked at the door like he expected him to barge in. "Who the hell do you think you are bringing him out here?" His eyes started to get wild with a fear that was settling in on him.

"He didn't follow me."

"I hope you're right about that." Jimmy scooted up onto the table so that his feet hung over the floor. "Now, are you going to help me like I paid you to do, or are you just going to let that killer come get me and Daniel?"

"Is the pisspot looking for me too?" Daniel wanted us to think he was too tough to be scared about it, but I could see otherwise.

"I didn't say that."

"Well, a horse can crap on him," Daniel said. "And on you too, for bringing him here. What about that poster, Jimmy? What did you do to get on it?" Daniel might be mad at me, but he wasn't happy with Jimmy now either.

"The poster again. I'm sorry you mentioned it, Sonny. Don't either of you Injuns understand that don't matter now? Hell, for all we know, the marshal is outside and all you want to do is talk about some poster."

"What are you saying, Jimmy? Is there a reward on you or not?" Daniel didn't have much patience at the best of times, and he was wearing thin now.

"I'm saying we can talk about the damn poster later. Right now, one of us needs to go out and look around like you said."

"Why don't you go?" Daniel glanced at the window. I knew he wanted to go check, but gun or no gun he wasn't so crazy about walking out blind into the dark.

"Because you got the eyes for it. I don't. Hell, without eyeglasses, I can't even read the damn newspaper half the time."

I didn't remember Jimmy wearing eyeglasses.

Daniel shook his head. "And what if he's out there? Do I just shoot him?"

I felt my heart pick up. As mad as he was getting, I was afraid he might do that. I started to say something, but Jimmy did first.

"He's not out there. And even if he was, you damn sure wouldn't want to shoot him. God in heaven, Daniel, it's me he's after, not you. Just go check. It'll only take a second. Make sure nobody's bothering the horses."

Daniel twisted up his lips like he was sneering at that idea, but he was just acting tough for Jimmy's sake.

"Those your horses?" I asked Jimmy.

"Yeah," he said, looking at me again. "Bought them in town at a good price. Thought I'd fatten them up and sell them. Your brother let me board them here for a spell."

I looked at Daniel to see what he thought of that story, but he was still nibbling at something else. "And we ain't done talking about that poster."

Jimmy held up his palms. "Okay. But you're getting me so jumpy I can hardly think. Just go look, would you? I'll tell you after you come back."

"First I got to say something," Daniel said. "I don't like this, not being told things, Jimmy. We need to get things straight between us." He gave me a look. "Alone, I mean."

Jimmy nodded. "You're right. You're absolutely right. Let's talk later after he's gone." He jerked his head at me. "I'm sorry for acting uncivil. I'm your guest here and you deserve better from me."

Daniel nodded at his phony apology and then turned on me. "And you stay out of my doings. Stay out of my way."

"I'm just worried, Daniel. I don't want to see you get crossways with…"

"Who are you to be acting a mother hen to me? Hell, you'd still be in that school's jail if I hadn't come broke you out."

"Yeah, and I'd do the same for you, but I don't want to have to."

"You don't have to do anything for me, Sonny. It ain't your problem. Jimmy and me got a business deal here, that's all. So let it be"

"I can't, Daniel. You're my brother. His kind of business can cause you trouble."

"Hey, wait a minute, kid," Jimmy said.

"You're taking his money too, so I guess you're no one to talk," Daniel said.

I didn't say anything to that because he was right. He came over and put his finger to my face.

"You stopped being kin to me when you quit being Indian. Get on back to your whores and your little white girlfriend and leave me alone."

Bruises or no, I raised my fists. Jimmy jumped off the table and stepped between us. "Hold on. There's no use in that. We're on the same side here." He pulled me away and looked at Daniel. "Come on now. We need to cool down a bit. Go on outside and look around."

Daniel glared at me a second before answering him. "Get done your talking and get him out of here." He walked over, picked up the shotgun and opened the door. He shot me a last look, then pushed his hair over his shoulders and went outside.

As soon as he left, Jimmy looked at me. "What are you doing that for? Why are you so riled up?"

"What do you think? Because you're going after that payroll just like you always do."

He shook his head as if he'd already tried to explain but I was too thick to get it. "Okay, so I've done some things I ain't proud of..."

"The poster says you robbed banks."

"...but I won't do wrong by your brother." He looked at the floor. "I told you I got mixed up with some bad folks. I've been paying for it since." He looked up, playacting the part of the prodigal sinner. "But even back then, we didn't hurt honest folks. We took what the Yankee bankers stole from us in the first place."

"So you were getting back at the Union? Like Jesse James? That war's been over for forty years."

"Jesse James?" He tilted his head and laughed at that. "You think I'm like Jesse James?" He almost couldn't stop laughing. His eyes even started to water. He seemed real proud of my comparing him to an outlaw. "Well, some might say so for sure, but Jesse James was a gunslinger. Hell, I don't even carry a gun."

I had never seen him with one.

"So how many banks was it?"

Jimmy surprised me by getting serious again. His face tightened up and he lowered his voice. "Listen, Sonny, you've been around. Didn't those years at the Indian school teach you anything? The government don't care about little people—white or colored. It's run by Republicans who praise Jesus on Sundays and rob folks of all they got the other six. They don't care a fart in a whirlwind about what you or I want."

He was right about that. The Christians at Carlisle tried to take everything they could from me. They didn't even let me keep my name.

"Hell, just take a look at that breakwater they're building out there. You know how much that thing cost? Eight million dollars, that's how much. Eight million. Can you imagine it? And the government pays for it by stealing from you and me and calling it taxes."

I never paid taxes and I bet Jimmy never did either.

"The people here don't need that breakwater. It's for those codfish who run the mills up in Philadelphia. And they're the ones who run the government. It's their boats they're spending our money to protect."

He was getting worked up about it. I could almost believe he meant it.

"And look at that marshal," he said. "He goes around killing hard-working cowpokes and gets away with it. Why is that? Because he's a U.S. Deputy Marshal. That's why. Now that's a good government job for you. Killing folks."

"So you were like Robin Hood?"

"Like who?"

"Nothing."

"Jesse James was a killer. Shot a lot of men dead like your marshal did. I swear one thing to you, kid. I never killed anyone. Your marshal can't say that."

"But what about the payroll, Jimmy?" I needed to get him off his stump and back to business. "Are you going to steal it or not?"

He looked me straight in the eye like I saw a preacher do once. "No. I am not."

"And whatever you are up to, you'll keep Daniel out of it?"

"If Daniel gets himself into trouble, it'll be his doing, not mine."

I wasn't going to give him a chance to talk around this. "I want your word on it. You'll keep Daniel out of it."

"You have my word on it." He stuck out his hand.

It wasn't worth much, but it was all I was going to get. I didn't take his hand and we stayed eye to eye a bit more.

"So you going to help me or not?" he asked me.

"You want me to help you steal it?"

He laughed again. "No. I mean with the marshal."

That was the last thing I wanted to do. "I told you I'm done doing your errands."

"You're the one person can keep him off my behind."

"I don't care if he's on your behind, Jimmy. I care about my brother."

"Then keep him off me for a little longer," he said, meaning the marshal.

"Why should I?"

"Because I'm leaving town tomorrow. I promise you that. And then you and your brother both won't have to bother with me. But I have to cover my tracks first so the marshal can't follow me again."

Leaving tomorrow? That I'd pay to see. "And you'll leave Daniel alone?"

"I said I wouldn't get him in trouble. I still need his help getting a last few things done—unless you'll do them for me."

"You're leaving tomorrow?"

"I am."

"What about those horses you're fattening up?"

"Well, I can't do that now, can I? I'll see if I can sell them back."

I watched his face. He looked at me like an honest man asking for a simple favor. If he was leaving town, anything I did to hurry him along was worth doing. But I didn't trust him. I was still pretty sure he had some plans for that payroll.

"I'll try and get you some time. But just until tomorrow afternoon. No more."

Jimmy clapped his hands. "I knew I could count on you, kid." He slapped me on the shoulder.

Daniel wouldn't stay away from him unless he was forced to. I could think of one person who could do that.

16

By the time I got home and put the mare up, it was after midnight. It rained on the ride back in and the air was still soggy. The clothes Margaret had hung out were flapping around like ghosts in the dark yard. I wondered if Miss Lil had lent their owner some trousers or if he'd gone home in his long johns. I thought about going down to the Ocean House to see the marshal—he'd likely be playing cards at that hour—but I decided not to. I was tired to my bones and I wasn't up for more talking. The house was dark, so I went into the back room and flopped on my cot, hoping to get a couple hours sleep.

I woke up when the mare grumbled out back. I don't know what time it was, but the sky wasn't light. I thought at first I'd forgot to towel her down, but I remembered doing it. I got up and went to the window to look. Somebody was outside pulling those clothes off the line. With the shadows, I couldn't see who it was. It didn't look like Margaret. It was definitely a man, probably a client who'd stayed upstairs with one of the girls until his clothes dried out. Still, why wouldn't he just wait until the sun came up? I went back to bed and slept like the dead for the rest of the night.

The next morning was so grey you could barely tell outside from in. One of our roosters decided it was morning, though. I woke up to watered-down light leaching through the window. As soon as I opened my eyes, I tried to get up. But my back got a spasm and I flopped down a bit. The whipping Mr. Dodson had laid on me had caught up. My arms were raw where I'd covered up my head, especially along the back. My face stung just from splashing water on it. Still, the swelling had gone down and my color was coming back. Once I got started, nothing hurt so bad to keep me from doing what I needed. No one was up yet, but Margaret, bless her, had set out clean clothes for me the night before. I worked into them and sort of hitched out to the kitchen. I should eat something, but I wasn't hungry, I considered breaking off a hunk of cheese for later but skipped that and went out the door. A clingy fog had set in. The day was dreary as ashes and it had chilled down overnight. I was pretty anxious to get going. I didn't know who else would be up and about at the Ocean House, but I was betting the marshal would be.

He was sitting in the dining room with his back to me eating breakfast—potatoes and gravy, fried eggs and a slab of steak. I went over and stood behind the chair opposite him. He broke off eating and looked up at me, his fork halfway to his mouth. The smell of steak made my mouth water.

"You look a mess," he said. "You eat yet?"

I shook my head. He cut off some meat, folded it inside a piece of bread and held it out. I took it. I didn't like owing him favors, but my stomach didn't seem to mind just then.

"Jimmy do that to you?"

I shook my head again.

"Looks bad. Who then?"

"Doesn't matter. It ain't bad."

"Dodson. He seemed right upset with you."

I looked away. He pointed to the chair with his fork. "Sit down."

I looked around. Except for a woman in a corner looking at her coffee, we were the only ones in there. I pulled out the chair and sat. He scooped a forkful of egg and put it in his mouth.

"Jimmy didn't show last night," he said between chewing.

"You didn't come get him either."

He held the steak with his fork and cut another slice. "How would you know? You weren't there."

I stared at him, but he didn't look up. He knew I wasn't at Miss Lil's last night. Had he called asking for me? Miss Lil wouldn't give him the crust off her toast, let alone say whether I was home or not. Maybe he followed me out to the farm just like Daniel feared he did. I didn't know what to say, so I decided to say nothing. He reached for his coffee and looked at me again.

"What do you want, Mr. Sockum?"

"I heard you're a killer."

He put down the mug and leaned back in his chair a little. "Jimmy tell you that?"

He tugged a cigar from his vest pocket, bit off the tip, put it on the dish and stuck it in his mouth. He dug a match from another pocket and lit up, took a long puff and let the smoke drift up from the tip. He stared at me the whole while, like he was deciding what to say to put me in my place. His face didn't show anything, though. His eyes didn't even blink, but they shifted away a second or so and then back again.

"You heard right." His words were smooth and flat, like a spill of gravel.

"And you shot some cowboys. Gunned them down."

"They murdered my brother."

"Is that what marshals do?"

His eyes went away. "That's what brothers do."

I almost said something smart but thought better of it. I let it sit a while and then asked, "Why did you come here?"

"Because I'm looking for Jimmy."

I didn't let that go by. "That doesn't sound right. The *Pilot* said you were in Arizona."

He stared hard at me. "You said you heard about me. So when were you talking to Jimmy? Last night? Or do you just like hearing people read newspapers?"

I realized I'd said too much, so I shut up.

"I was in Arizona. I crossed Jimmy's trail. He was calling

himself Ryan then. His gang had robbed a train and were heading east. I followed after him."

"Picking up a scent don't mean you need to chase it. Why didn't you just stay out there?"

The folds around his eyes got tight. I guess he'd had enough of my mouthing. "Well I sure didn't come to jabber with you about my business. Now why don't you answer my question, son? What do you want?"

I wasn't finished, though. "You made it my business, didn't you, running me around with your messages? If you tracked him all the way from Arizona, I guess you can find him now. Why are you bothering with me?"

He took another long puff on the cigar. "You know what you're up against here?"

I stared at him. Hannah's father wanted to kill me and Daniel was in trouble. What else was there to know?

He took a long draw from his cigar and then rested the hand holding it on his knee. The smoke, grey as the rain, drifted up around his hair.

"Your friend Jimmy's planning to rob Dodson's bank."

"He's not my friend," I said.

"The Army boat came in yesterday. You see it? The one with the guns?"

"Course I saw it. It comes down here every month."

"It's carrying payroll for the breakwater contractors."

"So what?"

"They'll transfer it to the bank today."

I shrugged. "They've been doing that the last four summers."

"Ryan wasn't here when they did it before. I know how he works."

I shrugged as if none of that made any difference to me. "Why would somebody try to rob the bank today? There'll be police and soldiers everywhere." It was the question I'd asked myself a couple of times since last night.

"Same reason most do. He wants the money." He lifted his hand and took another pull on the cigar. "And it's a game for him too.

The more the risk, the more fun he thinks it is. Believe me, son. That's his plan."

I was getting lightheaded. "How can you know that? You've only been in town a couple of days."

"It's my business to know."

So there it was, standing buck-naked in front of me. It wasn't just me imagining things. I couldn't keep pretending anything Jimmy told me was true. And Daniel was right in the middle of it. I sat back and didn't argue with him. He just looked at me. I remember watching the smoke drift out around his mustache and up along his nose. My body throbbed like it had a headache. I let it boil over.

"If you got it all figured out, why don't you leave me alone? You're the marshal. Go tell the police about the robbery and collect your reward. Let them stop it." At least Daniel would be safer that way.

His cigar had burned down almost to the nub. He flicked off the ash and crushed it out under his boot.

"I talked to them and the mayor too. They don't want trouble from me, especially with regards to Miss Lil or her friends. They made it clear I'm not welcome here."

"So I guess they weren't stirred up by the reward poster?"

"They said it's a different man."

"How about the Army?"

"They don't talk to nobody."

I almost laughed. I felt misused the last couple of days, so I was happy he was too. "So now you're stuck with an old poster and a robbery nobody believes in."

"And with you."

"Me?"

"Yep. You're gonna help me find him first."

"Help you? Why should I do that?"

"Oh, the police will be plenty interested in my story after it happens. But it'll be too late then. For you too."

He'd said something like that before. "What does that mean? Even if you're right, what's it got to do with me?"

"With you and your brother both working for Jimmy, you think everyone will look the other way?"

"What's my brother got to do with this?" My stomach sank. I already knew the answer to that.

"Daniel. That's his name, isn't it?"

I felt my face go white. He knew his name. "What about him?"

"You know what he's up to." He eased back in his chair. "Your brother's helping Jimmy. He's paying him to do the dirty work."

"You're just crazy. You don't know anything."

"I'm sorry, Sonny. I do. I told you. It's my job. You know I'm not lying."

No. He wasn't lying and I knew that. So how much else did he know? Did he listen outside the cabin? That couldn't be. He wouldn't have let Jimmy leave, would he? Maybe he told the police about Daniel, though. I made myself calm down. "What do you want?"

"You came to see me. What do you want?"

It was my turn to look down. "I want to keep Daniel out of it."

He leaned forward and put his arms on the table with his hands clamped together.

"So he is planning to steal the payroll."

I looked at him. "He gave me his word he wasn't. He said he just wants to leave town."

"But you don't believe him."

"I don't care about him."

He nodded. "You help me get him and I'll try to save your brother."

That wasn't much, but it was more than Jimmy offered. I didn't answer, though.

"What's their habit for moving it?" he asked.

"Moving what?"

"The payroll. Getting it to the bank."

"The chief sends a wagon and a couple of police down to the pier. They load the payroll and then one drives while the other rides guard. I thought knowing things was your business."

"The Army send soldiers along?"

"I've never seen them."

"They come down the beach?"

"Yep. Along the beach road and then up South Street. Only way to get there if you take a wagon."

"Always at the same time?"

"No. They do it at different times, change it around. They're not stupid."

He pulled out a watch and flipped it open. "Bank opens in a couple of hours. Won't be before that."

While he was looking at the watch, I said, "Why do you care about Daniel anyway? Just let them get robbed. The mayor and Army will believe you then. You'll get all the help you want to catch him."

When he didn't answer me, I figured it out. "The reward. That's it, isn't it? If the Army takes him, you'll get nothing. But if you do collect, you'll leave. So what happens to my brother then?"

He looked at me. "Son, I don't plan to let Jimmy rob the payroll. But if he does, and if your brother's part of it, I can't help him. If you want to keep Daniel out of it, you need to help me get to him. We ain't got a lot of time."

That was true enough. If there was no robbery, then Daniel couldn't be arrested. I didn't trust Jimmy to keep him out of it. He didn't care about Daniel. In fact, he didn't care about anyone but himself. If it came down to it, he'd be the first and only one he'd save. It seemed once the marshal got his mind set on something, he was determined to see it through. So I knew he'd keep after Jimmy until he caught up with him whether I helped or not. The marshal might be old, but he was dangerous. I knew he wouldn't lift a hand to help Daniel either if doing that got in his way of that reward. I needed to stay close to him if I wanted Daniel safe. And at least he hadn't lied to me—not yet.

"I'll help you," I said.

The marshal pushed his chair out and stood up. He grabbed his coat and hat from the chair next to him. "Then show me the places somebody would hide three or four saddled horses."

17

We stood in the road outside the hotel. The wind off the bay had scattered the fog, but the clouds still hung low. It wasn't raining but the air had a chill to it. It didn't bother me, but the marshal looked cold. He stuck his hands in the pockets of his big canvas coat.

"Which way?"

"What are you looking for? There're lots of places with horses. We've got stables all over town."

"I said hide, not board. It'll be outside but hidden away so people can't see them."

I looked down the beach road. "There's woods all along there. Nobody goes over that way much." I hoped that included Daniel.

He followed where I was looking. "It won't be that way. There's no way to get out without crossing over the creek. I think it'll be closer to town."

I turned to him. "Well, town's pretty much filled with people. I don't know what you expect to find there."

He studied the road, following its track from the Iron Pier down the beach and coming up past us and turning up toward town.

"It'll be along the path the payroll wagon will take—no more than a mile off it and on a straight line into town. Somebody'll be there tending them." He pointed up South Street. "Where's that road go, the one that crosses this one on the other side of the bridge?"

"It passes in front of some pilots' houses and then goes out to the farms."

"Any of them abandoned?"

"One...sort of," I said. I was thinking of the Hickman place. It was a couple acres that ran into a salt marsh, not real good for growing.

"Sort of? Is it or isn't it?"

"It belongs to a towner who never stays there. He leases it out to colored folks from time to time."

"Any buildings?"

"A small house and barn."

"What's around it?"

"Not much. It backs up to the creek."

He nodded. "Take me there."

I didn't move. "If you're looking for Jimmy, try at his hotel. You know where he's staying." I was half afraid it would be Daniel doing the horse tending.

He stared at me. "You think because you saw me at breakfast that I just got up? He ain't in his hotel. He's too smart for that. Come on, son. Show me this farm." He started heading toward town.

I walked to catch up. "How do you know there'll be anything there?"

"I know how Jimmy works." He didn't look at me. "Where were you last night?"

"That's not your business."

"I talked to the colored woman who works at your house. She said you went out."

I doubted Miss Lil would let him talk to her, so he must have caught Margaret out in the yard. I hoped she didn't blab on me. She generally didn't say much to strangers. I didn't say anything else for a bit. I was trying to find out if he was testing me.

"I went into town."

"Go to see that banker's daughter?"

"What's it to you if I did?"

"Is that how you got whipped? He caught you?"

"No. I didn't see her or him."

He shook his head a little. "I don't think he takes well to an Indian courting his daughter."

"I'm not courting anybody."

"Uh-huh."

"What do you care?"

"I don't. I was checking to see if you'd tell me the truth."

He was testing me, but it didn't seem like he knew where I'd been. I wasn't about to tell him about our farm. He didn't need to go snooping around out there.

"You want my help or you just want to be nosy? What's this got to do with finding Jimmy anyway?"

"Nothing, I guess."

"Nothing," I said.

As we crossed the bridge, I looked down at the waterfront and spotted Tommy Dallard. He looked up and I waved, but he looked away and walked off. I didn't think much of it then. We came off the bridge and turned left—away from town—and started down the rutted road that ran along the creek. I glanced up, trying to spot the sun through the clouds so I could figure the time.

"It might be getting late," I said.

"Might be."

"Aren't you worried the robbery will happen while we're wandering around out here?"

He pulled out his watch. "We still got time."

"But we're going the wrong way."

"You know that, do you?"

"I know the Army's not taking its payroll out to some farm."

"I'm not looking for where they'll do it. I'm looking for where they'll wait."

I stopped walking. "Wait for what?"

He stopped walking too and looked at me. "To commence the robbery. They'll gather there with the horses ahead of time. A couple of them will work their way down on foot, I think, and hit that wagon as it comes up the road, probably right after it crosses that bridge. That'll keep them on this side of the creek and the Army on the other. The guarding will be weakest too when those policemen get close to town."

"On foot?"

"Yep. Too much confusion with horses along."

"What about the policemen?"

"What about them? I've seen your police. They don't look tough. And there's only two of them. Jimmy will take his chances. His men will have guns."

Guns. I imagined them pointed at Daniel. All he had was a knife. I couldn't see Officer Hickman getting himself killed over someone else's money, though.

The marshal pointed along the route from town in the direction we were headed. "They'll drive the wagon down this road to the farm, then switch the money to their horses and go hell bent for leather out of town."

"What if there's soldiers too?"

"Then they'll let it pass by and wait for another time to try. But I'm guessing Jimmy already knows if there'll be soldiers along."

"How would he know that?"

"'Cause he always studies the places he robs. Sometimes he'll hang around a couple of weeks figuring out what's what and how to do it."

Jimmy had been in town every bit of that. It pained me to think of the times I ran his errands, helping check things out for him as it turned out.

"Surprise is his card, son. He'll come where you least expect it. And when he does, it'll be a hellfire. It'll happen so quick no two people will agree on it later on."

He started walking again and I stayed beside him. He'd spent a lot of time studying things too. It almost sounded like he admired Jimmy.

"Won't the police get horses and chase after them?"

"They will, but that's another of his tricks. He knows how hard a horse can be rode before it wears out, and he knows that the law will do just that to catch up to him. So I'm sure he has fresh horses stashed somewhere. He generally hides them about ten miles down the road so when his mounts give out he can jump onto fresh ones. By the time the law catches on, they're stuck with worn-out horses and Jimmy's far away."

My stomach turned over. That's why Jimmy had horses at our cabin. I thought about telling the marshal about the horses, but I knew he'd go riding right out there and wait. He didn't care about the robbery, only about finding Jimmy. If I was going to help Daniel, I had to keep it from happening.

"Maybe we should go back. That wagon might be coming early."

"Sonny, I know you're worried about your brother, but it won't do us any good to wait at the wrong place. Banks and police and the Army all work off schedules. They won't be coming early. We need to find the spot. If I catch them there, I can stop it. Let's get a move on."

I didn't have a better answer, though I was certain Daniel would be there too. From the way the marshal talked, there might be a whole bunch of them out there. I walked along with the taste of my stomach in the back of my mouth.

We followed the road along the creek past a working farm to a place where the road turned farther inland. A narrow horse path split off there to follow the creek. I could see the washed-out roof of Hickman's barn through the trees.

"That's it," I said.

He didn't say anything. He turned off and headed down that way with me behind him. The farm was on a patch of land set against a line of trees with a one-room farmhouse out front and a small field in the back. It was out there by itself. The path wandered past it, then petered out to a trail into the woods. No one was living there, nor had been for some time. The house's door had worked loose from its hinges and was leaning out like a drunkard.

"This's the place," he said. "Stay out here while I have a look around."

His hands were in his pockets and that worried me. I looked down at his coat. There might have been something in there.

"You got a gun?" I didn't want him shooting Daniel either.

He looked back at me. "A gun takes away choices. You don't want to have to shoot someone just to defend yourself."

"What if they have guns?"

"Keep your head." He straightened and stared directly into my eyes. "You get in trouble, watch the face. You'll know if somebody's going to pull the trigger. You'd be surprised how you can think if you don't get excited."

"What good will that do you if they shoot you?"

"Shooting and hitting are different things. Most who get to shooting are too excited—maybe scared, maybe angry. They yank it out and start blasting. Damn hard to hit anything in that state. Jimmy won't shoot me, though. He's smarter than that and he's careful."

"What if he does?"

He turned and started walking away again. "I didn't say I don't have one, son."

He walked through the yard to the house, checked in the windows and then started around to the back. He stayed close to the wall as he went until he could look around the back without being seen. I feared for what he might find back there, but I couldn't stand and do nothing if Daniel was there. I thought about what he said, took a deep breath and followed him into the yard. I crept along to the back edge of the house wall and didn't hear voices, so I took a chance and peeked around it.

The marshal was alone. He was squatted down, scratching through the thin grass with his fingers.

"They're not here," I said.

"I told you to stay back." He straightened up and looked at me.

"Is this the wrong place?"

"No. This is it. Those are Jimmy's boot marks or someone small as he is. He tramped all around out there. Inside the barn too. Probably yesterday from the looks of it."

"Are we too late?"

"Shouldn't be," he said. He pulled out his watch again and glanced at it. "Let's get back."

"Back? I thought you were going to wait here and catch them."

"They ain't here. They should be."

"Maybe it's off. Maybe the Army decided to ride along."

"Maybe. I need to hire a horse." Without looking to see if I was coming, he headed out to the front. I caught up and grabbed his arm.

"You can't stop it, can you? You just want to be in on his capture."

He pulled away and stared at me. "There's something funny here, son. I think he's put a turn on it."

"What about Daniel?"

"If he's part of it, he needs to fend for himself. If I were you, I'd stay clear."

He walked away from me again, taking long strides to hurry back to town.

"You're the one who talks about brothers," I shouted. "You don't care about him. But I do."

I took off running past him and didn't look back. I had to find Daniel and I could only think of one place to look just then.

18

The waterfront, a two-block section on the town side of the creek, was a jumble of rusted junk, an abandoned shipyard with rotting boats and a dilapidated stable. I don't know why the town never got around to cleaning it up. Rundown clapboard houses had been slave quarters before the war, and a broken stone wall was all that was left of a fort long gone before most people in town were born.

Sometimes Tommy Dallard stayed in that stable. Tommy's daddy worked a farm just west of town. Daniel sometimes stayed out there with them when he didn't want to ride to our place. Or couldn't. Tommy didn't take much to hard labor either. He was past forty and still living at home. When his liquor ran low, he'd steer at the piers for the hotel whores like I'd seen him doing the day the marshal came in. Then he'd get drunk again until he was broke.

I guess it was the marshal's talk about Jimmy's gang that got me thinking. By himself, Daniel didn't make much of a gang. But throw in Tommy and a couple more idlers and you might have one. Tommy was the closest thing Daniel had to a friend.

Tommy was down there, moseying around and doing nothing. He was wearing workmen's clothes—plain pants and a blue shirt. I picked my way down along the wall and traipsed though the mud past a broken axle missing a wagon to the old stable. I was half-afraid to go inside. I squatted down and pried away a broken slat. It was dark and smelled of wood rot. I had to shade my eyes to see in. The barn was empty and there were no tracks in the sodden hay that covered the floor.

I squatted there somewhere between relieved and discouraged. Because Jimmy and Daniel weren't in there, I hoped the marshal was wrong about the robbery. But seeing Tommy dressed like he was lurking around down here was not a good sign for certain. I got up, brushed the mud off my pants and tried to think of some other place they might hide out. I was halfway back up to the street when I heard somebody shouting—two men going back and forth at each other. I heard a wagon coming over the bridge above me, and when someone cursed and then a gun went off, I took off toward it.

I came up the embankment to the bridge road and saw Tommy Dallard again. He stood on the side closest to me with his back pressed against the handrail. He'd tied a white kerchief over his nose and mouth, but it had slipped down a little. He had the shotgun he hunted with, and he was pointing it at the wagon. He looked nervous. His eyes were flickering around like he was expecting somebody else to show up. He was breathing hard too like he'd been running, and sweat circles under his arms turned his shirt dark.

Two policemen sat in the wagon. One was Officer Hickman. They didn't look much like police just then. They huddled together, barely moving, watching Tommy. Their hands were half-raised and their eyes looked like pans of fried eggs. Officer Hickman's shirt was wrinkled, and his shirttail stuck out the side of his pants. He looked like he'd been roused early that morning. The driver, who I didn't know, held the reins in the air too as if he was praying over them. A pistol hung from his belt, but he didn't look like he wanted to use it. Officer Hickman had a rifle draped across his lap with the barrel pointed out, but he acted as if he forgot it was there. The wagon was a small-wheeled one with a square bed and low sides. A big spotted horse was hitched up front and it stood still like it was resting. It was old and well-worked and either too lazy or too tired to look back at the commotion.

"Get out of there," Tommy shouted. He waved the shotgun like a parade baton, showing them where he wanted them to go. Officer Hickman and the other one looked at each other as if Tommy had said it in Chinese.

"You won't get away with this," Officer Hickman said finally, though from the way he stammered he didn't sound like he believed that.

Tommy jerked the gun stock to his shoulder and aimed it at the other policeman's head. "Get down now. I mean it."

His eyes looked wild. He glanced off to the side again to see if anyone was coming up on him, I guess. I was, but he hadn't seen me. His kerchief slipped all the way down and was draped around his neck.

I heard some whispering behind me, but I didn't look. Some people were shuffling around back there. I guess they came running when they heard the gunshot, but none of them seemed anxious to be noticed just then.

"I'll shoot your head off, you son of a bitch," Tommy yelled.

That seemed to convince the policemen. The driver brought his hands down in front of him to show he wasn't going for his pistol and then scuttled down on his side. Officer Hickman lowered his rifle too and gave Tommy a "don't shoot" look as he used his fingertips to push the rifle off his lap onto the footrest. He raised his hands again and stepped down from the wagon, keeping his eyes on Tommy the whole while.

"What do you want?" Officer Hickman asked. It didn't sound like he really wanted an answer.

Tommy looked past him. "You. On the other side. Come around the back, slow, and keep your hands raised up the whole time."

The other policeman moved to obey. Tommy rushed to the wagon, pushed Officer Hickman to the side, slapped the shotgun onto the seat, and climbed up beside it, grabbing for the reins. Officer Hickman never lowered his hands. I moved out to the middle of the road to block Tommy's way.

"Tommy. What are you doing?" My hands were up too. I didn't want him shooting me.

He looked up at me. He looked confused and angry all at once.

"You part of this? Where the hell you been?"

"What?"

"Quit gawking and get up here." He had the reins raised in both hands, ready to slap the horse.

"Where's Daniel?"

"Oh, Christ." He spotted the people behind me. "Get the hell out of the way"

He slapped the horse hard. Its head jerked up, surprised, but it didn't look back. It lurched forward, moving faster than I'd ever seen it move. The wagon wobbled as it started up, coming at me. Tommy pulled at the horse to get around me and fell back onto the seat for his trouble. I jumped away to the side as he went past.

"You're worthless as he is," he cursed at me

He pulled himself up and whipped the horse another time. The wagon clattered down off the bridge, slanting over toward Gills Neck Road. A group of maybe six or seven towners standing out in the road, one woman among them, scattered like a set of tenpins when they saw him coming.

The marshal was there too. He was standing on the sidewalk across from me, right at the corner. He must have just got back to town. He didn't run. He had his own pistol out. He pressed his back against the side wall of a river pilot's house, raised the gun in his right hand and braced it with his left. Tommy saw him too. He ducked and yanked the horse to the left as hard as he could. The front wheel left the ground as he swerved into the corner. The marshal stepped back a little, avoiding the terrified horse, but he didn't drop his aim. The wagon righted itself and barely made the turn, with the marshal's pistol following it all the way around. Tommy strained to stay in the wagon and just hold on. He squatted low on the seat, trying to avoid the marshal's aim and get away from there as fast as he could.

The wagon stopped weaving back and forth and the horse settled into a panicked bolt down the middle of the road. The marshal waited what seemed like a long time, his eye sighting along his right arm, and then he pulled off a shot. I saw the flash and heard the pop. I looked to see if he got Tommy. I couldn't tell from where I was, but the wagon didn't slow down.

I ran down off the bridge, heading the same way.

"Stop that boy," one of the busybodies shouted, calling to the marshal I guess. "He's one of them."

The marshal stepped out into the road and grabbed my arm as I went past. His left hand grabbed me and he wheeled me around like a kid's top.

"Wait. You can't catch him."

"Let go of me." I twisted away and broke his grip. Or he let go of me.

"I'll get a horse," he said.

"I don't care about him," I shouted. "It's Daniel."

He dropped his hands and let the pistol hang at his side. "I'll give you what time I can," he said, "but I'm coming out there after him."

I took off running again, chasing the wagon and Tommy.

19

By the time I reached the place where the path split off to the farm, the wagon was around the bend and out of sight. Its wheels clattered though deep ruts and the traces slapped and clinked. It seemed like Tommy was going to get away clean and I was relieved. The marshal was wrong about everything. Tommy robbed the payroll by himself—or maybe with Jimmy's urging—but Daniel wasn't part of it. I decided to go back to town. The marshal and the police could go chasing after Tommy for the money. I didn't care about it.

I'd gone no more than a couple of steps when I heard something thrashing behind me and I turned around. Someone or something moved through the high weeds that separated the road from the path down to the old farm. I went closer to look. About a hundred feet away, I saw Tommy break out of the weeds and take off half-running toward the farm. He grunted and cursed half under his breath as he ran, and he moved in a kind of shamble, like a tethered horse or a hunched-back old man. He'd slung a leather satchel over each shoulder—hanging on to them by the tie-ups—and his shotgun was tucked under one arm. I could see from the way he was struggling the bags were heavy.

Piss on him. He must have tossed the bags over the side and jumped off, leaving the wagon to run on by itself. It would be some while before anybody would catch up with it. The road went straight for another five or six miles before it turned, and that horse could run a long way without a driver.

I waited until Tommy was further down the path before I started after him. I didn't want him spotting me before I knew what he was up to. When I got in sight of the farmhouse, nobody was in the yard. I guessed he'd gone around to the back, so I worked my way around the house, careful to be quiet. I still hoped he was alone, though I wouldn't have been surprised to find Jimmy. There was nothing back there either except the field and an old barn. Timbers had rotted through and fell in, leaving a big hole in the barn's roof. The field had no fence. It had gone fallow and wild grass and weeds overran it.

I started toward the barn, but a horse chuffed in the trees at the back of the field. I couldn't see it, but the grass was flattened in a wide swath going back there, wide enough a horse could have made it. He was down by the creek. A commotion started up on the main road now too, horses huffing and men shouting. It sounded like the police and whoever else had made it that far. From the sounds of it, there were lots of them. They all moved by in a rush, following the wagon down the road. If that draft horse wore out too soon, they'd all be coming right back. I ran across the field, ducked between the pines and looked out through the stretch of marsh grass that lined the back of the field. A strip of sandy loam ten feet or so wide had been rough cleared by someone and flattened near the creek. Tommy stood there, and my brother was with him.

Daniel had on canvas pants, a shirt the color of old leaves and boots with metal spurs that I'd never seen before. His hair was bound up into pigtails and pushed back over his shoulders. Three horses were tied to a scrawny scrub pine not far from where I was. Their muzzles were covered with handkerchiefs to keep them quiet. The biggest horse was a nut-colored gelding with a coal mane and a white blaze. It was a fine animal and costly, not the one he kept at our farm for working. The other two were brown mares as fit as the gelding. They might have been the ones I'd seen hobbled at our farm the night before. But it was dark then, so it was hard to say. All three were saddled in good leather with wide canvas bags tied across their rumps.

Daniel and Tommy were down the way a bit from me, facing each other. The Army payroll satchels, bulging like potato sacks, lay near their feet. Tommy huffed like an old hound. One hand splayed over a blood splotch on his pants leg—I guess the marshal got him—and the other held his shotgun like a walking stick. Daniel had his feet apart and his arms spread. The two of them looked like they might come to blows. Neither had noticed me.

"Where the hell were you?" Tommy shouted at Daniel.

"Waiting for you," Daniel shouted back.

"Waiting? You were supposed to be helping me."

"No I wasn't. I had the horses."

"Well, nobody told me. I was there by myself, for God's sake." He kicked at a satchel and didn't look like he believed him. "It all but went to hell. Good thing it was them town police. They about shit when I pointed this at 'em." He jiggled the shotgun. "They jumped off that wagon and started running."

"What about that?" Daniel nodded at Tommy's hip.

Tommy glanced down as if he'd just noticed it and pulled his hand away. "Hell, that's nothing. One of them towners found his spine. Fired off a few rounds, must've nicked me. I didn't feel nothing. I was too burned about you not showing up."

"I wasn't supposed to be there," Daniel said again. His right hand fidgeted a little.

Tommy noticed it and rolled the shotgun up so it pointed at him. "I don't give a god-damn about supposed. I coulda used some help and you wasn't there."

Daniel slapped the barrel away. "It was you that messed up. You probably were at the wrong place."

"Oh, I was at the right place, all right. But your brother showed up instead of you."

"My brother? What's he got to do with it?"

"Nothing god-damn useful that I could see. He was worthless as you are."

Daniel scowled. He was worked up over what Tommy said and he was getting both confused and provoked—not a good mix for him. Tommy stared him down a second and then glanced at the marsh grass as if he expected someone to come crashing through it.

"The hell with you," Tommy said. "I'm getting out of here and I'm taking these with me." He kicked the satchel again. "You ain't getting cowshit as far as I'm concerned. I'm the one got shot."

Daniel's hand twitched again, and I thought he might grab for the shotgun. But he bent over his boot and pulled out the long-handled hunting knife he kept in there. I'd seen that look on his face before. His rage now had him past worrying what Tommy could do to him.

"You ain't going anywhere, Tommy. I'm getting my piece."

Tommy took a step back, probably thinking Daniel might come at him. Daniel just squatted down and slashed at the pouch. It must have been made of a special weave because the blade skidded off it like he'd struck a rock. He didn't seem surprised, though. He started working the blade at the lock and chain that bound the top. Tommy figured out what he was doing, and his eyes got wide.

"Hey. Leave that alone."

He pointed the shotgun down at Daniel's head. I saw Daniel's eyes shift a little and his knife hand bunch up. I think Tommy might have fired. He was so mad he wasn't thinking straight, so I stepped out of the high grass.

"Stop it."

Tommy's hand jerked and I thought he'd pull the trigger. But he spun around and turned the gun on me.

"Now you show up."

He thumbed at the hammer and I scrambled backward and fell onto my butt. Daniel's head came up too and he saw me. He stopped prying at the payroll bag and stood up slowly, moving to the side a little so he could watch both me and Tommy.

"What do you want, Russell?"

Tommy looked at Daniel and then back at me. He kept the

shotgun pointed at me. "That's what I want to know. Shit, Injun. You coulda got me killed back there."

"The police just rode by out on the road," I said. "They'll catch up with that wagon and come right back."

"God-damn it. What are you doing here?" asked Daniel.

"I came in town just before the robbery. I was down at the waterfront looking for you."

"Came on it? That's bullshit. You and that marshal were messing around, weren't you? This is his doing, ain't it?" He gestured at the payroll bags with his knife.

"What marshal?" Tommy looked at Daniel. "Nobody said nothing about a marshal." Things were spinning out of hand for him and he wasn't one to handle it. "What the hell are you two up to?" He shifted the shotgun a little toward Daniel again as if he couldn't decide which of us was the bigger threat. Daniel ignored him.

"I didn't do anything to you," I said. "I'm trying to help. Anyway, he already knows about this place." I knew as soon as I said it that I shouldn't have.

"You sorry bastard." Daniel's hand came up and the knife pointed at me.

"We ain't got time for this," Tommy said. He looked around again like he expected the police any second. "Forget the god-damn kid. Let's take the money and get the hell out of here." I guess he decided Daniel was due some after all.

"There ain't no money," Daniel said to him, still watching me. "You messed up, Dallard."

"What are you talking about?" Tommy stepped past Daniel and looked down at the satchel. He lowered the shotgun and his face got dark as a squall. "I'll be god-damned." He bent over and reached into the bag and his hand came out holding sand. He let it dribble between his fingers as if he was hoping it would change back. "What the hell is this?"

Daniel crouched down next to the second bag. He flicked the knife at the chain, and it popped off like it wasn't fastened. He pried at the canvas and then pushed the bag over with the mouth of it toward me. Even from where I was, I could see what was in it. Tommy looked at Daniel as if he thought he'd made the switch somehow, but my brother only looked at me.

"You son of a bitch."

Then the light hit Tommy too. "You bastard," he said, aping Daniel's words. He raised the gun again. I ran for the creek and jumped in just as the gun went off. I don't know how close he came, but I heard the buckshot spray past my ear. The creek was shallow, but the bed was thick with mud. I plopped into it up to my chin. I floundered, trying to get up before he got off another shot.

There was no need. Tommy dropped the shotgun and ran over to the horses. The shot spooked them, and they were twisting around, yanking at the reins and trying to free themselves. Tommy pulled the gelding loose and the mares came untied too. He scrambled up like he had a bull on his tail and the horse writhed and tossed its head. Tommy dug in his knees and slapped the reins hard. The gelding bolted and Tommy nearly slipped off. He righted himself and the horse took off out of there with Tommy clinging to its back. I heard them crash through the tall marsh grass, heading back through the farm to the road. The other horses scattered, which left Daniel and me staring at each other.

I got myself upright and standing, still in the water.

"Who the hell do you think you are?" Daniel's voice was low and flat now. He came toward me, half crouched, with the knife pointed toward me. "You're all white now, ain't you? Don't give a damn about blood."

"No, it's not like that." I backed up, sloshing and stumbling to get away from him.

"Sure it is. You think 'cause you got a white girlfriend and work in that whorehouse, I'm nothing."

"That's not true."

"You don't even want Jimmy giving me a piece of something, do you? You think 'cause he's white, that's yours too."

He waded into the creek, moving toward me like the mud wasn't there.

"I don't care about Jimmy, Daniel. I don't care about the money."

"Well it ain't there, is it? So what'd you do with it? That marshal promise to split it with you?"

"No. I don't know where it is. I thought it was there." I had my hands up, but I nodded and half-pointed at the payroll bags.

"Yeah, sure you did. I oughta gut your lying white belly."

He came at me and swung for my head with the back of his knife hand. I tried to duck it, but I was too slow. His fist caught my eye and I went to my knees again. I tried to push up but slipped and went sprawling. I could hear his legs sloshing as he came for me again.

"Daniel, I swear I didn't..."

He slammed the butt-end of the knife on top of my head and I went all the way down. I swallowed some water and gagged and coughed it up.

"You're just lily liver now, Russell, ain't you? You're not my brother. You're a white bitch dog."

He stepped across me with one leg and put his boot square on my back so I couldn't get my face up. His spur dug into my back. He used his weight to hold my face down under the water. I was near to drowning by then and frantic to get a breath. I struggled and squirmed under him, splashing behind me to try to grab his leg, but I only ending up thrashing. Suddenly his weight lifted off and I rolled over onto my side, gasping. I pushed up onto my elbow, slipping off it in the mud and thinking he'd be staring down at me. I couldn't see for the muck in my eyes. I wiped them with my sleeve and looked around. Daniel lay crumpled onto his side in the creek a few feet away from me.

"He's all right," someone said. I knew the voice and looked for it.

The marshal stood over me with his pistol in his hand. Up close it looked heavy—maybe two or three pounds. I couldn't imagine holding it steady enough to hit anything. He had his lips pressed together, which made his mustache puff out. He was watching me, probably waiting to see what I'd do next. I looked at my brother again.

"I buffaloed him," the marshal said. "It'll bleed a little but it's not serious. Get up. We need to get you out of here."

"Why did you hit him?" I was mad at Daniel, but madder at the marshal.

"He had you in a fix."

"That was between us. I don't need your help."

"Get up, Sonny. If anybody heard that shot, they'll come rushing on back here." He grabbed my shoulder and yanked me to my feet.

"Leave me alone."

He shoved his pistol into his coat pocket and went over to squat beside Daniel. He poked around his head where he'd hit him, pretty much the same place Daniel had hit me. "He'll come around in a bit." He stood up again. "Where's Jimmy?"

"There's nobody else, just Daniel and…that other one." I was no friend of Tommy's, but I didn't want the marshal asking me how I knew him. I got up and went over to Daniel. His chest was moving in and out and a gouge cut into his head. His arm was half-folded across his chest and his hand hung open. The knife wasn't in it. The marshal walked around, looking at the boot and hoof prints in the mud.

"He wasn't at the robbery either," the marshal said.

"Who?"

"Jimmy."

"Maybe you got it wrong." I didn't care where Jimmy was.

"No. This is his work. Something is going on. Let's go, son. We don't have much time."

"You need to go. Go on. Leave us alone."

"If you stay here, you'll be saying your brother was one of them."

I didn't understand. It must have showed, because he said, "We''ll take him along. We'll need to carry him. Right now, the police know about the one who hit the wagon. They come back and your brother's not here, they won't know different."

Carry him? He weighed two hundred pounds. Where did the old man plan for us to take him? "Aren't the police with you?"

"They went chasing the wagon. I rode out here by myself."

"Why?"

"To find Jimmy."

"There's no money," I said.

That stopped him. He looked at the sacks. "What's that?"

"See for yourself."

He walked over to one of them and squatted down to look. "The other one that was here—Dallard—he run off with it?" If he knew Tommy's name, the police did too.

"No. That's the way they were."

The marshal grunted, but it was more of a laugh. He looked inside the other satchel and shook his head. "I'll be a son of a bitch." He stood and came back over. "They switched it." He grinned as he said it.

"Who did?"

He looked at me like the question was a puzzle to him too. "I don't know. Somebody. Looks like they outfoxed him."

By him I guessed he meant Jimmy. The money caused everything that was wrong with Daniel, and now it wasn't even there. "Where is it?"

"That's a good question. Maybe still on the Army boat. Maybe it's already at the bank."

"So there was no robbery?" Which meant Daniel hadn't really done anything wrong.

"Well, we ain't found the money. So until we know better, there's twenty thousand dollars gone missing. And someone tried to rob it, so the police will stay after them 'til they're caught."

"But if it is missing, they'll think it was Tommy Dallard."

"And you," the marshal said. "People saw you on the bridge and Dallard talking to you. So did the police."

I didn't say anything, but I looked at Daniel again. If I had just stayed out of it like he asked me too, he'd be away safe with Tommy now.

"Wasn't your fault," the marshal said. "You tried to warn him."

I got mad again, but only at Daniel this time. He was going to drown me over a sack of sand. "Robbing the Army and going to jail for it. It's fools' work."

"Nobody's in jail yet far as I can tell. And you might keep him out if you stop jawing and get a move on."

"Why are you helping him?"

"Because you helped me."

One of Daniel's pigtails had come undone and was spread over his face. He still wasn't moving, but his eyes flickered a little like he was trying to open them.

"Where're we going to put him? In the barn?"

"They'll search there." He looked to the other side of the creek. "Let's get him over there, into the high grass or trees."

We'd have to get across the creek, which was mud at the bottom and up to my shoulders in the middle. "Then what?"

"We get back to town. Find out what happened to that money."

"I'm not going in there."

"Think you better. They're looking for you too. You need to explain things."

"Explain what? Tell them it was Daniel, not me?"

"Tell them what you want. Just be sure they know you weren't part of it. I'll back your story if need be."

"What do you care?"

"I told you—because I owe you, son."

"You don't owe me anything. I'm not leaving him." I didn't want the marshal's help, but I couldn't get Daniel out of there by myself.

We'd have to get him across the creek and the woods were beyond that. I didn't know how we'd manage it, but I was determined Daniel wasn't going to jail over a sack of sand.

"How're you planning to move him?"

"Carry him."

I went over and stood behind Daniel. I crouched down, reaching below the water to take hold of his armpits. The marshal came over too, but when he reached down to grab his legs, Daniel's eyes opened.

"Who the hell are you?"

"Steady, boy."

Daniel twisted away from us, rolled over, pushed up onto his elbows and looked at me. There was disgust in his look. He tried to stand up and I stepped toward him, ready to help him.

"Get away from me."

He was wobbly and he put his hand to his head, as if doing it would make the pain go away. He looked at the marshal next.

"I asked who you were."

"I'm the one keeping you out of jail."

Daniel blinked a couple of times and then stood up fast. He twisted around and fumbled at his boot, trying to find his knife. The marshal held it up for him to see.

"You liar." He meant me.

He bunched his fists and staggered into me. I fell backward into the creek again with Daniel on top of me. I pushed him off and before he could come at me again, the marshal cocked his pistol. I stopped moving and Daniel did too. We both looked up at him. The Colt was pointed right at Daniel's gut.

"Next time I won't use the barrel. Get on out of here."

Daniel didn't answer but I saw anger in his eyes. He stood and stared at the marshal for so long I thought he might try charging him barehanded. Finally, he broke it off and stood up.

"The hell with you."

He slowly brushed mud off his pants and shirt as if he had the whole day to clean himself up. I wanted to try to talk sense to him, but I saw he was past arguing. He held out his hand.

"Give me my knife."

"Not today," the marshal said.

Daniel shrugged as if it didn't matter and dropped his hand. He looked at me then, holding my eyes like a snake on a mouse. "We're not done."

"Daniel."

He jerked his head like there was nothing more to say and turned away.

"If we get out of here now, no one will…"

He wasn't listening, though. He waded further into the creek like he was going for a swim, but then he kept on walking across it. He climbed out on the other side without looking back.

"Daniel."

He took off running. When he reached the trees, I lost sight of him.

"Give this to him when he's cooled down," the marshal said. He held out Daniel's knife and I took it from him. "I'm going back to town. I suggest you do the same."

"I'm not going."

He shrugged almost like Daniel had. "You see Jimmy, you tell him I'm coming." He turned away.

The last thing I cared about was Jimmy, but something came to me while I watched Daniel go. Whoever it was decided Daniel should stay with the horses had kept him out of things, whether they meant to or not. If it was Jimmy, then I guess he thought he'd kept his word to me. But it still had put me and Daniel at odds and almost got me killed.

"If I see him, I'll tell him," I said to the marshal's back.

20

Daniel was gone again and there was no sense chasing after him, seeing as he blamed me for what happened. And besides, no one was looking for him now. I didn't want to go into town, so I decided to head back to Miss Lil's. I was looking for Jimmy. I was certain he was behind the botched-up robbery and I wanted to know why he mixed Daniel up in it after he promised he wouldn't. I wasn't keen on explaining to Miss Lil why I'd taken off with the mare the night before or what I'd been doing that morning, so I hoped I wouldn't bump into her. I wasn't sure how I would manage that, but Margaret solved it all for me. As I came around the back, she was carrying a basket load of folded laundry inside.

"My land, Master Sonny. You're all a mess again," she said when she saw me. "Was it Mr. Dodson did that to you?"

She was wearing the same brown dress and white apron she had on the day before, which meant she'd been there all night.

"No. I...fell in the creek. Is Jimmy here?" I told her the truth, just not all of it.

"In the creek? What on earth were you doing in there?" She put the basket on the porch and came over to me. "Here, let's get you inside and get those wet clothes off you."

"I'll be fine," I said. I stepped around her and rummaged through the laundry basket, pulling out a dry towel and one of my shirts. I considered taking a pair of pants, but I didn't want to go inside to change and sure wasn't going to in front of her. My hands came away leaving black, caked creek mud all over her clean laundry. She'd have to start over on that load. But I give her credit. When I pulled off my filthy shirt, she took it and dropped it on top of the pile like it belonged there.

"Margaret, have you seen Jimmy?" I asked her again while I toweled myself off. "It's important."

"Why, you just missed him. He got here first thing. Spent the morning sitting in the kitchen, eating breakfast and talking with Miss Lil. He left not long before you got here."

I looked out at the beach road. "How long ago?"

"Oh, maybe a half an hour."

I pulled on my clean shirt. It was sticky. It hadn't dried all the way hanging in the damp air. Sticky or not, it was warmer than the one I took off.

"What was he talking to Miss Lil about?"

"Oh, this and that. He was waiting for Miss Anne to get up."

"When was that?"

"You mean Miss Anne? Why, she's still sleeping."

"Asleep? At this hour?" It was nearly noon. Miss Lil didn't like her girls sleeping in late on weekdays.

"She's tuckered out for certain, poor thing. The three of us were up all night looking for her gentleman's clothes." She meant Miss Lil and Anne and herself, I guess.

"What happened to his clothes?" I tried to remember who was with her last night.

"Somebody took them. Something had got spilt on them and I offered to clean them off a bit…while he wasn't wearing them, I mean." Her face got a little red. "I washed them and put them out to dry. When I went back out to get them, they weren't there."

"What did he do?"

"Well, he had to stay 'til we found them. He couldn't very well leave in his long johns."

I stepped back and looked up at Anne's window. "Is he still up there?"

"Oh my, no. His clothes finally turned up. I came out looking one last time this morning and there they were, folded and stacked as nice as you please on the porch. It was just before the sun came up, so I guess whoever took them had a change of heart when he saw he had an Army man's uniform."

"Captain Sweetland," I said.

Margaret nodded. "Off that Army boat. Even after we found his clothes, though, he didn't seem in any hurry to leave. I could see that Miss Anne was dead on her feet by then, but he just wanted to sit up there jabbering with her. Miss Lil didn't shoo him off, though, since we'd lost his clothes and all. He finally left when one of those soldiers came looking for him, talking about a robbery or some such. Miss Lil asked Jimmy about it, but he didn't know. So she went into town to see for herself. Did you hear anything about that, Master Sonny?"

"Uh, no. I didn't."

"Well, it certainly got Captain Sweetland agitated. He tore right out of here half-dressed. He went scampering out the front door in his stocking feet and carrying his boots."

"When was that?" It had to be well after ten.

"Oh, I don't know, Master Sonny. I don't pay too close attention to the time. It was before Mr. Jimmy left, though. He was still in the kitchen having himself a laugh listening to the whole thing. Miss Anne never came back down, though. I'm certain she was asleep before Captain Sweetland reached the front door."

"And what time did you say Jimmy showed up?"

"It must have been seven o'clock or so, I guess. Captain Sweetland was still dawdling in Miss Anne's room at the time."

Jimmy showed up at seven and left a little while before I came. That meant he was there when the robbery was going on, and he'd made sure Miss Lil would attest he was there the whole time.

"Did Jimmy say where he was going when he left?"

"No. But I got the feeling he was planning to leave for good. He told me to make sure I told Miss Anne he said goodbye."

That corked it for me. Whatever Jimmy had been up to, he had to leave town. For some reason, he'd taken Captain Sweetland's uniform off the line and then put it back. And though I didn't know why, I was certain it was connected to the sand in the payroll bags. And I was ready to bet he knew where the real money was.

"When Miss Lil comes back, tell her I'll be back later," I said. I turned and started back out to the beach road.

"Where're you going, Master Sonny? Miss Lil's concerned about you, coming in so late and then being up and out early this morning."

I didn't look back. "I'm going to find Jimmy and tell him goodbye."

21

The marshal might have thought Daniel was out of trouble, but I knew better. If those police ever caught up with Tommy, he'd blab to save his neck and they'd know Daniel was in on it too. My only thought was to find Jimmy and have him turn over the money so they'd stop looking for it, though I didn't have any idea how I'd get him to do that.

I went into the Breakwater Hotel looking for him and told the man at the desk I had urgent news for Mr. Lowe. He didn't want me in there, of course, but I pestered him until he told me Jimmy wasn't there. He hadn't checked out, though, which meant he was still around somewhere. I got let down a bit when I thought he might be hiding out at our farm because I didn't have any way of getting out there. But since Tommy had scattered the horses and Jimmy was on foot when he left Miss Lil's, I decided he was probably close by. Besides, the next ferry would leave at two o'clock and I was pretty sure he'd want to be on that one.

I didn't want to go up into town because the police were looking for me too. But I didn't see much other choice. Right after he came to town, Jimmy put some money and things into Mr. Dodson's bank for safekeeping, so maybe he'd gone back to take it out.

I went over the creek by way of the old footbridge on Market, right next to the waterfront. I didn't want to cross at the South Street bridge where there was a lot of traffic and someone might see me. I came up the alley beside the old jail and took a peek out at Second Street. The first thing I saw was the marshal. He stood on the sidewalk a few feet away with his back turned to me. I could hear somebody shouting. That's what the marshal was looking at. I stepped out onto the sidewalk using him to block any view of me and looked over his shoulder.

Mr. Dodson came charging out the bank's door like a train out of a tunnel. "You're a god-blamed liar," he barked at somebody behind him. I could almost see steam rising off his bald head. He was moving pretty fast for a man who walked stiff legged.

A short man in a blue uniform and thin as a crabapple tree came out behind him, catching the door and pushing it open again. His Adam's apple looked like a knot on a limb, and his face was set like he was concentrating on something important. He walked strong and straight-legged like soldiers do, but his manner was undone by the way he'd got dressed. The buttons on his coat were one-off up the front so his collar ran up on one side. His shirt wasn't tucked all the way in either. A white tail flapped over his seat as he went. The bank's door banged closed.

"Let's see what the mayor has to say about it," Mr. Dodson shouted.

Another man came across the street to meet them. He was a towner for certain. The day had started to warm, but he was wearing a grey suit with the vest buttoned and a bow tie that bunched at his neck. He looked to be about the same age as the marshal, but he was thinner and clean-shaven, and his clothes were a sharper cut. I guessed he was the mayor. Miss Lil had spoken of him quite a bit, but I'd never had occasion to run into him.

Mr. Dodson went right for him. "This is an outrage, James. This ignoramus thinks I have the Army's money." He waved at the man behind him without looking at him.

Other people were about too, huddled in little clusters. A robbery in town was unheard of, and this was in broad daylight.

Though only a few of them had seen it happen, I'm sure the gossip about it had spread like sand blowing. Several of them perked up at the ruckus going on in the street. I guess after missing the robbery, they hoped they might get to watch something else.

"Calm down, Henry." The mayor sounded more agreeable than his face seemed to be. He looked over at the Army man. "What's this about, Captain?"

Mr. Dodson waved his arms. "I tell you what it's about. This moron is lying to cover up his ineptitude."

The mayor's expression didn't change but I could see he was getting irritated. "I said calm down, Henry." He pointed to his side. "Please. I want to hear what Captain Sweetland has to say."

Mr. Dodson put down his hands, but he didn't calm down any. I had moved up next to the marshal. I wanted to ask him about Jimmy. He nodded and stepped to the side for me to see. He put a finger to his mouth to tell me to be quiet.

Mr. Dodson was turned away from us, but Captain Sweetland saw the movement and glanced at us. I'm sure he didn't recognize me, but I knew him right away. He looked away again.

"You know him?" the marshal asked me, not looking over.

I nodded. "He spent the night at Miss Lil's. Comes around every month when the Army boat's in."

"All night?" He looked at me. "Looks like he got dressed in a hurry."

"Someone stole his clothes off the clothesline. He didn't get them back 'til this morning. That's what I need to talk to you about."

The marshal frowned and went back to watching Mr. Dodson and the others. "Let's hear this out first."

Captain Sweetland was standing near the mayor now. "Mr. Dodson claims he can't locate the payroll we delivered, sir," he said as if he was reporting on an underling to his superior officer.

Mr. Dodson went at him. "Claims? I don't have your damn payroll and never did."

The mayor put out an arm to hold him back. "I don't understand, Captain," he said. His voice was firm but skeptical. "The payroll was stolen. Someone held up the wagon carrying it in here this morning."

"No, sir. Only bags of sand were stolen. I had one of my men deliver the real payroll to Mr. Dodson's bank this morning."

"You're a damn liar," Mr. Dodson shouted.

"What? Why would you do that, Captain?"

"We got word there might be trouble, so we made the switch early, before sunrise. We loaded the police wagon as a decoy to cover us bringing the money in here a different way. And it's a good thing we did, sir."

I was amazed at how much scheming and switching Captain Sweetland could manage from up in Anne's room.

The mayor's head tilted back a bit, like somebody'd taken a swipe at his face. "We thought the robbers made the switch." He turned to Mr. Dodson. "Is this true, Henry?"

Now Mr. Dodson looked like he'd been punched. "True? Of course it's not true. They didn't bring any money in here. They had it stolen from under their noses and they're trying to cover it up with this lame-brained story."

The captain held his ground. "Sir, my man handed that payroll money over to one of your clerks." He looked as unhappy as Mr. Dodson was.

"Oh, for God's sake."

The mayor frowned at him. "I said cool off, Henry. The captain's made some serious claims. Instead of going on like this, why not just prove him wrong?"

"Prove him wrong?" Mr. Dodson stared at the mayor like he thought he escaped from a madhouse.

The mayor raised his hand. "Have you talked to your clerk? Maybe you missed something in all the confusion. Let's all go inside and get to the bottom of this."

"What's the matter with you, mayor?" Mr. Dodson brayed the last word. "The payroll's been robbed. My bank has advances out to the contractors. A lot of them. If the money goes missing, we're the ones on the hook. Why aren't you helping that worthless police chief of yours catch the real robbers instead standing here accusing me?"

"The police are hunting for them now." The mayor used his calm voice. I was impressed he could stay cool with all of that going on. "But if Captain Sweetland says there was a switch…"

"I don't care what he says. Look at him. He looks like he just climbed out of bed."

Mr. Dodson didn't know how true that was. Captain Sweetland flushed. He looked down at his shirt. From the look on his face, he just discovered how badly he had gotten dressed. He struggled to act offended while he unbuttoned and rebuttoned his shirt. He reached behind and stuffed in his shirttail.

"James, this philistine lost my money."

The captain frowned and stood up straight. I don't think he knew what he'd been called, but he was sure it wasn't good. "There's no call for that, sir. Besides, why would robbers take time to fill the payroll bags with sand?" He asked this question of the mayor.

"That's a good point. Why would they, Henry?"

Mr. Dodson threw up his hands. "Search his boat, mayor. Search his belongings. He probably stole it himself."

The mayor shook his head. "Make up your mind, Henry. If the money's not in your bank, then either the robbers took it or the Army has it. It can't be both."

Mr. Dodson started flapping his arms like he might fly off at any minute. "Oh, for heaven's sake. How did my bank get to be the villain in all this? We were robbed."

The mayor shook his head and looked at Sweetland. "I'll get to the bottom of this, Captain, but I'm quite disappointed in the Army's behavior here."

The captain's jaws went slack like he'd swallowed something sour but didn't want it to show. "Uh, I don't…"

"If what you say is true, you used our police wagon to draw the robbers away from the real payroll."

The captain looked like a scolded schoolboy. "Uh, yes, sir. We did. We were trying to…"

"There's no excuse for that, Captain. There was a robbery. My policemen could have been killed. And the Army knew about it and didn't lift a finger."

"But we did, sir. We protected the payroll."

Mr. Dodson couldn't take any more. "Horse manure. His story's a damned lie."

"No need to be vulgar, Henry," the mayor said, and then to Sweetland, "I plan to contact General Gillespie personally and express my displeasure."

Captain Sweetland tensed but didn't say anything. I think he saw it was turning against him and decided not to make it worse. I'd like to see him explain to that general what he was doing the night the payroll was getting robbed. Especially if his men were asked about it too.

The mayor looked at Mr. Dodson. "Okay, Henry. Let's just go inside and have a talk with your clerk. Meanwhile, Captain, don't leave. Keep your boat tied up at the pier until I tell you otherwise."

Sweetland nodded, but he looked so uncomfortable I was guessing he'd do otherwise. Mr. Dodson came to life again. He wagged his finger in the mayor's face. "My bank's been robbed and you're picking daisies."

The mayor wasn't about to lose control of things. He took hold of Mr. Dodson's shoulder and turned him toward the bank. "If I find I've been lied to, I'll not rest until the Army makes good." He prodded him to start walking. "But right now, you and I are going inside to take a look at things."

That might have been the end of it except when Mr. Dodson turned around, he spotted me. He pointed his finger again. "There's the black boy that did it. Everybody saw him."

I turned around to run but the marshal grabbed me. "Let me go."

"The boy had nothing to do with it," the marshal said.

"Don't you call me a liar." Mr. Dodson kept on coming. He rolled up his fist and was on top of me before I could pull away. The marshal was quicker. He yanked the revolver from his pocket and brought it down on Mr. Dodson's shoulder next to his ear. He went down on the sidewalk like a bag of leaves and stayed there. I found out he was a lot braver beating up kids.

One of the town men saw what happened and started over to help him. Then he looked at the marshal and thought better of it. The mayor came up and stood right in front of the marshal. "What do you think you're doing, sir?

"Get this hooligan off of me," Mr. Dodson moaned. "Put 'em in jail, both of them."

"He ain't hurt," the marshal said. "I don't take well to people beating up kids."

The mayor's eyebrows flicked up and down. He must have heard what Mr. Dodson had done to me the day before, but he gave the marshal a hard look.

"We don't allow firearms inside town limits. That's the second time today. Give it to me." He held out his hand, palm up.

"Maybe you should start," the marshal said. He stuffed the Colt into his pocket.

The mayor dropped his hand but didn't back off. "I'm placing you under arrest, marshal."

"I don't think you are, mayor." He put his hand on my shoulder and turned me around. "Let's go, son." We started walking back the way I came in.

"Do something," Mr. Dodson squeaked behind us. "Don't let them walk off."

"I'm sending the police around for you," the mayor called to the marshal's back.

"We need to find your friend Jimmy," the marshal said to me.

22

"You came into town to tell me that Army fella lost his uniform?"

I knew he didn't think that was my reason. We were headed down South Street toward the beach again. Though the sun was showing through the overcast in spots, the clouds were low and the breeze was chilly when it kicked up. I could smell rain coming. The marshal walked so fast I had trouble staying up with him. I guess he wanted to get out ahead of the mayor and the police.

"I was looking for Jimmy. I just found you first."

"Because you figured out he took that uniform."

He was quick that way too. "I wanted to know why."

He glanced at me. "And now you do. He made the switch while your madam was entertaining the captain."

"He told the soldiers on the boat he was an officer."

"Had them fill the bags with sand and they let him take the money for safekeeping." The marshal grunted. "Smart son of a bitch."

"He'd have let Daniel take the blame for it."

"And that other fella. Still think he's your friend?"

I never did, but I was tired of saying it. "Where're we going? He's not at his hotel."

"The ferry's leaving soon."

"The ferry? He hasn't checked out yet."

"He ain't going to. How much money was in the payroll? Twenty, thirty thousand? You think he's worried about leaving his clean shirts?"

I wondered if Anne would go with him. She kept Sweetland tied up all night so Jimmy could get away with the money. She probably even spilled wine on him so he'd have to take off his clothes—not that he'd mind that. Anne had lied to me almost as much as Jimmy, and it hurt to find that out. I was a fool for setting her up high in the first place. That always was one of my problems. You'd think I would have learned.

We turned onto the beach road. The ferry had tied up at the Queen Anne's Pier. It was hard to miss. It was a big bobbing thing, long as three railroad cars, with a smokestack stuck through the middle. The marshal slowed down as we got near, and he stared at it like he was flushing a pheasant. It had two decks. The top one wrapped itself around the smokestack and a wheelhouse that took up most of the front. It was getting itself ready to leave. The engine huffed like an old nag and steam wheezed through the stack.

"You see him?" I asked.

He didn't answer, so I looked where he did. The last of the passengers were boarding and the rest milled around on the decks waiting to push off.

He pointed. "That's him, ain't it?"

The ferry wasn't full, but plenty of people stood on the decks. We were every bit of fifty yards away from it, but he'd spotted Jimmy right away. After he pointed, it took me a second or so of looking to find his moon face and scrawny mustache. He had on a short coat and a little round hat. He was on the top deck, leaning against the rail like a tourist, watching the last passengers get on.

"Yep." It occurred to me it was the first the marshal had seen him since he came to town. He must have recognized him from the wanted poster. I didn't see Anne.

The marshal pulled back his coat and fished into his vest pocket, taking out two silver dollars. He stuck his hand out without taking his eyes off the ferry. "Have the hotel hold my things until I send for them."

I stared at the coins. "Why? What're you going to do?"

He turned his head to look me. "Take them. They won't do it for free. I'm getting on the ferry."

I took them. He didn't wait for me to say anymore. He started off at a pace just short of running.

I called to him, "You coming back?"

"Likely not," he answered, without turning this time.

I watched him go, not knowing what else to do. I glanced at the upper deck again. Just as I did, Jimmy looked back at me. He must have seen the marshal too because he straightened up and took a couple of steps backward. I decided to get closer and watch what happened.

The pier's long hulk ran a couple of hundred yards out over the water. The ferry was docked a little way down it. Two straggling passengers were still working their way up the gangway—a young dandy in a grey suit and a fine-looking woman with hair bunched under a bonnet. A skinny man in a starched white coat and trousers gave her a wide smile as she handed him her ticket. The marshal stepped onto the gangway behind them, pulled back his duster again and dug for money. I looked for Jimmy again, but he'd ducked out of sight. The marshal handed the crewman some coins and got on. Then I lost track of him. Right after he got on, two dockhands pulled the gangway down and undid the lines. The horn let out one long blast and the ferry rattled and clanked and started to move away.

I wasn't happy about what Jimmy'd done, but at least Daniel was safe and the two devils I wanted rid of were going out of my life on one stick. I should have turned tail and that would have been the end of it. Instead, I went up the three wooden steps onto the pier. I had no plans to get on—they wouldn't let me on at any fare. I just wanted to see the marshal catch Jimmy. I hoped he'd give me a high sign or something. After all that happened, I didn't want Jimmy getting away clean. The marshal seemed like the only one left who could stop him. I was walking along beside the ferry, trying to spot them before it got past the pier, when Mr. Dodson came up on the pier behind me, moving faster than the marshal had.

"Stop the ferry." He fired a few shots in the air to get their attention.

I heard the shots, but I didn't look back right away. I guess I was too caught up in things to recognize his voice at first. He came running right past me, tall and skinny and so stiff-legged his body bobbed up and down. He didn't look my way.

"There's a criminal on board," he hollered to the white-coat crewman standing at the back. I assume he meant the marshal. The crewman crossed his hands in front of his body a couple of times and shook his head. The ferry was still close to the pier and not even halfway along it, but it was moving forward.

"You're too late. Take the next one."

Mr. Dodson ran up close to the rail and waved both his arms. "No. You didn't hear me. There's a man on there who's wanted by the police."

I'm pretty sure Mr. Dodson wasn't just made a deputy.

"I'm sorry, sir," the crewman said. They were barely a couple of feet from each other.

"Moron." Mr. Dodson favored that word.

The crewman turned away from him. Mr. Dodson looked around for someone else to set about. His eyes bulged, and his mouth worked like he was cursing to himself. He'd worked himself into a lather trying to stop the boat. By then, he and the mayor and the Army all must have discovered the payroll really was missing. I know he blamed me for that, and probably the marshal too. Now he thought we were getting away. Because Captain Sweetland claimed the money was delivered to Mr. Dodson's bank, I wondered if now the police thought one of the bank clerks was in on it. I suspect the captain didn't tell them otherwise.

Mr. Dodson didn't find anybody to help him, but he did spot me.

"There. There's the one." His mouth pinched in. He ignored the boat and came for me. "You thieving Indian. Where's my money?"

He was close enough when he turned around that I didn't have time to move out of his way. He came at me like a bull, crashing into me with both arms straight out and slamming me against the wooden guardrail.

"I don't have it," I sputtered at him, trying to breathe and talk at the same time. I clawed at his arms, trying to push him off me.

"Liar." He grabbed the front of my shirt with both hands, then stood up straight and lifted me off my feet and shoved me over the top rail. He was a lot stronger than he looked to be. He leaned hard into me and I went backward over the top with his face pushing into my chest. He leaned over so far he had to let go of me to grab onto the rail.

A dockhand saw it and shouted at him. "Sir, what are you doing?"

Mr. Dodson ignored him. He was too intent on pushing me without going in himself. To keep from going all the way over, I locked my legs around Mr. Dodson's head and squeezed. He gurgled once and looked up at me, half-snarling, and then grabbed my legs, trying to pry himself free. I was stronger than I looked too. It was too late for him. We'd gone too far over the rail.

All the movement and sounds and colors went flying from my brain and left behind some blurry photographs. In one of them, the rail is pressing into the small of my back and I'm rocking over it like a teeter totter, dragging Mr. Dodson with me. In the next, my head snaps back and I'm trying to untangle my legs from him. I can feel his fingers claw at my legs and shoes, but he can't seem to get a grip on me. Then my feet fly straight up over my head and I'm trying to walk upside down in the air. I fall headfirst and paddlewheel my arms as if that will stop me. The top of my head bangs into something and my neck bends forward. I twist and fold at the waist so that my feet are pointed down again and I'm looking at the pier. Mr. Dodson isn't there. My backside wallops into something like a wall. The force of that takes the breath from me again and it feels like I'm stuck there a second or two, held up by my surprise, I guess. And then time starts up and colors come back, and I slide down over the rough boards of the hull and head for the bay.

In all my flailing, my hands managed to find what I'd banged against and I grabbed for it. It was a line attached to a ship fender. Getting hold of it stopped my falling, but it jerked me up like a fish on a hook and I heard my shoulders crack. I craned my head looking for Mr. Dodson and saw him below me. The space between the boat and the pier was narrow, but he'd passed though it clean and went into the bay. He landed on the flat of his back and a big circle of water got pushed up around him. Then the ferry moved over him, and he was gone from sight. I'd seen someone else disappear in the water like that. It wasn't easy to watch no matter how much I hated him. But I had other things on my mind just then.

As the ferry gathered steam, I started to swing from side to side on the line like a clock pendulum. I twisted in the air like a smokehouse carcass. My arms throbbed like the dickens, but the ferry was moving fast. I was afraid if I let go, I'd get pulled underneath too.

I wasn't much of a swimmer, but I knew sooner or later I had to let go. I couldn't hang there all the way to New Jersey. I dragged my heels to stop swinging and bent my knees and pushed around to look at the pier. A couple of dockhands saw what happened and shouted for the ferry to stop. Between the engine's roaring and the clattering of the screw gears, I don't think anyone could hear them. Another one of them waited for the boat to clear the pier so he could climb down after Mr. Dodson.

The ferry started going faster. Rows of small waves from the wake moved under my feet. Whatever I was going to do, I had to do it quick. The pain in my shoulders was fierce and my arms started to spasm. The ferry rocked as it moved along and I started swinging again, beating up against the hull. The bay wasn't deep close to the shore, maybe ten feet at most, so if I dropped off and didn't get pulled under, I might be able to tread water until someone could throw me a line. But we'd soon move past the pier and then no one could get to me. I knew I should have let go, but right then hanging on seemed less scary.

The boat had slowed a bit and now the aft end drifted toward the pier. I closed in on a line of pilings as thick as trees. The ferry would hit them and bounce off—that's what the fender was for—

but the line had me wrapped around it. The pilings were about six feet apart at the water line and the waves smacked as they beat against them. If I let go now, I'd flounder there for sure. I twisted my head to look up at the boat rail. I hoped somebody had heard the commotion, but nobody was looking back down at me. The pier's wooden planks stuck out a few inches to the side. Maybe I could grab onto them just before we banged into it. But I wasn't sure I could even reach them, let alone climb high enough to keep from getting squashed. Still, those chances looked better than just holding on, so I decided to try for it. I shifted my hands and twisted so my back was to the boat and I bunched my legs to prop my feet. I fixed my sights on the nearest piling, which was closing in fast, and got ready.

"Sonny." The fender line jerked in my hands. "Come on. I'll pull you up."

I looked up again, forcing myself to take my eyes off the pier. The marshal's head was there now. One of the flaps of his coat hung down over the rail toward me like a window curtain. He held the line and heaved on it. I looked back at the pier and did some quick figuring. I was a half dozen feet down over the side, which was a long way for him to haul me, and I had no more than a few seconds before I got smashed.

"Hold on and walk up," he shouted. "Just get close. I'll grab you."

I might have been scared, but not so much I couldn't save myself. I swung around so I was facing up and started to scramble up. Someone on the pier shouted, "Watch out," which I took to mean I was short on time. When I looked up again, my head was still three feet from the railing. The marshal leaned over and stretched out an arm. I let go with my left hand and reached, but I was a couple of inches short. I swatted at his coattail instead and almost lost my grip, so I slapped onto the fender line with both hands and heaved for all I was worth. I felt him grab the back of my shirt. Then his other hand went under my arm and I let go and clutched the deck rail like it was the gate to heaven. The marshal reached over me to grab my seat and he yanked just as the ferry banged into the pier. It was like getting kicked by a horse. I came over the rail on top of him, then landed on my side and rolled onto my back. The marshal flopped backward too. I laid there a couple of seconds, catching my wind and trying to sort through what happened. There was mildew on the slimy deck, and I remember thinking how good it smelled.

The marshal pushed himself up and then gave me a hand. "What were you doing down there?" he asked me.

I took his hand and stood up. "Mr. Dodson came after me," I said. It took an effort to speak. I bent over and put my hands on my knees to catch my breath.

The marshal went over to the rail to look. "Where is he now?"

"He fell in," I said.

The marshal glanced at me and then back at the pier. We were some distance off by then. "I don't see him."

I didn't say anything to that. I thought he might call a crewman over or something—maybe tell him to turn the boat around—but he didn't. I guess he thought Mr. Dodson got out of the water okay.

Some of the passengers had gathered around us by then, milling and gawking. I expect that was more excitement than they'd seen in a while. One of the men was a towner I recognized, and from the way he prissed his nose, I don't think he was admiring my grit. None of them seemed happy at having me on board with them.

The face the towner made reminded me of Mr. Dodson again. If he drowned, it was because he was after me. However bad he'd been to her, Hannah would be alone. Her mother had left them, and I didn't know if she had other family nearby. Anybody who saw Mr. Dodson and me on the pier would run to tell her what happened, and they were sure to say I killed him. That would be easy enough to believe after the reports of him whipping up on me at the beach and later me holding up the payroll wagon heading for his bank. Even if I didn't get thrown in jail for it, I'd never see Hannah again. I panicked, thinking I should stay on the ferry to New Jersey and then make my way from there.

The towner stopped frowning and stepped forward. "What's he

doing here?" he asked the crowd. The marshal answered by glaring at him and he backed away. That brought me around.

"Where's Jimmy?" I asked. I started to fume about him again, since he caused all that happened to me.

"Hey, kid. Up here. You all right?" The marshal looked up and then I did. He was right above us, leaning over the upper rail. "That was a hell of a climb you made."

23

Jimmy looked down at me. "What are you doing with him? You're supposed to be helping me." He didn't look like he was too worried about it. That was too much for me. I took off running, heading for the outside stairs that led up to his deck.

"Wait, Sonny," the marshal called after me. "I'll take care of it."

I didn't, though. When I saw that big cat grin of his laughing at me like it was a joke, everything that had happened got pushed onto him. All I could think about was tearing off his face. Two crewmen were coming down the steps as I went charging up. One of them grabbed at me, but I pushed right through them like unchained gates. The one who grabbed me shouted and the other turned around to come up after me.

People on the top deck must had heard the commotion because they turned, staring my way when my head popped up the stairs. They scattered like hens when they saw me, though. With my torn clothes and bruised-up face, I must have been the savage they took me for, which was how I felt.

Everyone except for Jimmy, that is. He was still leaning against the rail with his back to it now. He had his arms crossed like he was waiting for a seat. He smiled when he saw me. But when I got to the top and kept on coming at him, his look switched over to surprise. He unfolded his arms like he wasn't sure what to expect. As soon as I got to him, I grabbed his coat with one hand and took a swing at him with the other.

"What the hell?" He jerked his arm up and caught my blow. From the way his lips pinched in, I knew I'd hurt him some. He rocked back and his hat flew off and flopped upside down on the deck. He tried to move to the side as I swung, so when my punch landed, the rest of me carried past him into the rail. I found my balance, pushed off, turned around and came at him again. He grabbed my arm with both hands before I could swing, and he pushed me away. I slipped on the wet deck and went down, but I scrambled up and started after him a third time. He held his hands out in front of him to keep me back, but I planted myself in front of him and kept my fists up.

"Sonny. Hold on. What's got into you?"

My body shook. I guess I didn't know 'til then how mad I was.

"You're a liar and a coward."

I spat a little when I shouted, and some landed on his face. "What are you talking about?" He wiped at his mustache and backed away a little. He wasn't grinning anymore.

"You…you said you'd keep Daniel out of it." My anger was so high I stammered.

Jimmy looked at me like I'd dropped out of the sky. "What are you going on about? Keep him out of what?"

"The robbery. That's what. Don't put on that face. You know what I'm talking about. You made a big show having them hold up the police wagon so you could sneak off with the payroll."

Jimmy frowned at me, acting like he was confused. That made me want to throttle him. If he said something like, "The payroll was robbed? Is that a fact?" I would have.

Instead, he just blinked a couple of times like he couldn't make heads or tails of what I was telling him. "Kid, that's just crazy."

"Don't play dumb, Jimmy. Daniel had the horses at the getaway spot waiting for you, but only Tommy Dallard showed up. And I know about Captain Sweetland's uniform."

He shook his head. "Whatever Daniel did, I had nothing to do with it. Last time I saw him was out at the farm with you. He had a job to do for me this morning…"

"Yeah. I saw him doing your job."

"He was supposed to take a buyer out to see the horses. Damn. I guess that means he didn't."

"You're a damn liar." I was going to go after him again, but one of the crewmen grabbed my arm and turned me around.

"Come with me, son." The crewman was an old, half-bald white man and I could have knocked him down, but the other one was young and beefy and looked ready for me to try. The marshal loomed behind them. I pulled my arm away. "What do you want with me?"

"You're not allowed on this boat. There's witnesses who said you pushed a man off the pier. We're locking you up until we get to Cape May. The police there can decide what to do with you."

Somebody saw us on the pier, but the crewman was acting like the only thing Mr. Dodson got was wet.

"He didn't push him," Jimmy said from behind me. "That man fell in on his own. I watched the whole thing happen from up here. He was attacking Mr. Sockum at the time."

The bald crewman gave him a look. So did I. "You know this boy?"

"I do, sir, and I'll vouch for him."

The older crewman didn't look happy. He looked at Jimmy and then at me again. "We don't allow Negroes on board."

"I'm a Nanticoke," I said.

"I don't care if you're Sitting Bull. No Negroes."

"Leave him…" The marshal stepped around the young crewman and came to my side. "He's with me."

The old man stepped back so he could look at all three of us. He made a face to show what he thought of defending me. "He didn't come on board with either of you. And it don't make no difference. He needs to be locked up or get off." He gave a half smirk when he said that, pleased with his own wit.

Now that they saw no one was after them, we started gathering a crowd of curious folks again. The marshal looked over at them and then back at the crewman. He pushed his hands deep into his coat pockets. I could see the bulge of his gun, and from his expression, so could the crewman. The marshal wasn't threatening him exactly, but his meaning was clear. "I said let him be."

The old man nodded at the marshal's pocket. "If that's a firearm, you can't carry it on board." A nervous wave passed through the onlookers when he said that, but he just shook his head like he couldn't believe what he had to put up with. "I'm going to see the captain. When I come back, I'll want that gun." He looked at me. "And I don't want to see him here when I do."

"I'll be here," the marshal said.

The old man grunted and started across the deck to the wheelhouse. The younger crewman shot us a look and followed him. For all his beef and clucking and scowling, it seemed like he had a lot less mettle in him than the old man.

I turned around again and saw Jimmy grinning at us. "Well, you must be the marshal I keep hearing about." He gave me a sidelong glance. "Is this what you call keeping him away from me, kid?" Before I could snap back at him, he stuck out his hand. "Pleased to make your acquaintance, marshal."

The marshal looked at him but didn't offer to shake hands. "Don't try rubbing snake oil on me," he said.

Jimmy raised his eyebrows like there was no accounting for how some people could act. He dropped his hand. "Well, I can see you've got your mind made up about me, don't you?" He looked at me and nodded at the stairs. "How about we all go downstairs? We can sit inside at least and get acquainted."

He smiled like we were all old friends or something. The nosy onlookers, maybe fifteen or twenty of them, hung around nearby watching. They could smell more excitement brewing. I heard the old crewman banging on the wheelhouse door on the other side of the deck. "Open up, sir. We've got a problem out here." Jimmy started for the stairs.

"Just stay put," the marshal said.

Jimmy looked at him like he said something foolish and funny at the same time. "Stay put? What are you thinking about, marshal? You plan to shoot me here?" Another murmur rumbled from the crowd.

Jimmy made to go around the marshal. The marshal's hand was still in his pocket and he nudged the Colt so Jimmy could see it move. He stopped and raised his eyebrows again. He didn't stop smiling.

"I'm taking you off this boat." The marshal didn't sound like he was asking for his opinion.

Jimmy laughed. "You crazy? You going to point that at me all the way to Jersey?"

"You ain't going nowhere else."

"That's so." He shrugged. "So at least I'll go get my hat." He spotted it stuck between the baseboards of one of the benches. He was lucky it didn't go over the side. He walked over and picked it up, swatted it against his pants and brushed it with his sleeve. When he put it on, he had a pleased look on his face.

"Got this hat in Fort Worth," he called to us. "Made of beaver. Cost me eight dollars. I wouldn't want to lose it."

He came back over to us. "So, marshal. Now what?"

I could see the marshal was bedeviled. Jimmy acted like he was no more nuisance to him than a horsefly, and it was working. The marshal wouldn't shoot him there, his threats didn't seem to trouble him, and Jimmy hadn't given him a reason to whack him over the head. I don't think he was used to being brushed aside.

Jimmy unbuttoned his coat—slowly—so the marshal wouldn't take him wrong, then slipped it off and tossed it across his shoulder like he was a dandy. He gave the marshal another look and walked away.

The marshal looked surprised. "Where do you think you're going?"

Jimmy went to the starboard rail and leaned against it, facing the water. The marshal followed after him. "You don't think I'll shoot you, do you?"

"If you do or don't, there's no need for me to pass the time staring at you, is there? You ain't much for conversation." He didn't look back as he said that.

I didn't know what to think. "What happens when the old guy comes back?" I asked them.

"Don't worry about him," the marshal said to me. That was easy for him to say. Jimmy ignored my question but half-looked back at the marshal.

"You planning to turn me in? In New Jersey, I mean?"

"That's what I figure."

"Hmmm. That's too bad. I got things I need to do."

"What you need don't matter to me."

Jimmy turned all the way around and leaned his backside against the rail. "What's the matter with you, marshal? Why are you so intent on this? You don't even know me."

"You got a price on you. That's knowing enough."

"It's hard to believe you came all this way for that. Ain't there any folks out your way with rewards on them?"

"I had my reasons."

"Well, they must be daisies." Jimmy watched him a couple of seconds and then said, "You know, I don't think this has anything to do with me. I think you went looking for trouble and then got restless when you couldn't find any. I was just an excuse you found to keep on moving. Must be hard for an old lawman to quit being one, eh? I'm out here minding my business, and you take it on yourself to come spoil it. What did I do to you to earn that kind of treatment?"

The marshal gave him a long look. I could see he was getting impatient. "Enough talk, Ryan. Seems like your business is other people's money."

"Ryan? The name's Lowe. Hell, you even got the wrong man."

"You're the right man," he said, "no matter what you call yourself."

It was time for me to butt in again. "We can't turn him over in New Jersey. We've got to return the money to prove that my brother's innocent."

"There you are, going on about that again." Jimmy shrugged

like he might have to give up on me. "Look, I'm sorry about your brother, kid. I really am. But I had nothing to do with that. Only a fool or crazy man would rob a government payroll with soldiers and police guarding it."

"Come on, Jimmy. You're saying it was just bad luck that brought you into town when someone else was planning to rob the payroll?"

"You can believe that or not, but I came here for one reason, and that was to spend time with Anne."

I don't know if I rolled my eyes, but I made it plain what I thought of his story. "You're not letting him get away with it, are you, marshal?"

The marshal let a couple of silent seconds go by and then said, "I don't care about the payroll, Sonny. That's the Army's problem. I'm turning him in for the price on his head and then I'm done with it."

"But my brother..."

"Your brother was part of it whether you like it or not. Giving the money back won't change things. Dallard is the only one can tie Daniel to the robbery. Just let things be and hope he don't get caught."

The door to the wheelhouse opened and a skinny, clean-shaven man in a white suit stepped out. He wasn't the captain. I knew them all. He talked to the older man a minute and looked at us a couple of times. Then both of them came over to us. The younger crewman wasn't with them. He must have stayed inside.

"What's this all about, sir?" the new man asked Jimmy, evidently thinking he was the only gentlemen among us.

"Why, not a thing, Captain," Jimmy said, intentionally inflating the man's rank. "We're just taking in the air and enjoying some conversation."

The man looked at me but kept talking to Jimmy. "We don't permit colored on the ship."

"Well then, everything is fine. Sonny here is a full-blooded American Indian."

"That's the same as colored in our book," the crewman said.

"Is that a fact? I'd say your book is out of date."

"And I'm told he's been fighting. We'll have to hold him inside and put him off when we reach New Jersey."

"He won't be happy, Captain," Jimmy said, though he didn't seem inclined to stop them.

The older crewman got tired of Jimmy's banter. "This other one has a gun in his pocket, Mr. Spikes," he said.

Mr. Spikes turned to the marshal and stuck out his hand, sort of like Jimmy had earlier. "Turn it over to me, sir. You can have it back when we've docked."

"I don't believe I'll do that," the marshal said.

"That's not acceptable. Our policy is no loose firearms on board. Please hand it to me. Now."

Mr. Spikes kept his hand sticking out, but the marshal didn't oblige him or say anything more. Finally, Mr. Spikes blinked and lowered his arm, not certain what to do next. He turned to the older man. "Take this colored boy to the lifebuoys room, Mr. Bayles, and lock him inside."

"Yes, sir." The old crewman stepped over to me and grabbed at my shoulder. I pulled away and stepped away from him.

"Don't get smart with me, boy," Mr. Bayles said. "It won't go well for you." He moved toward me again and raised his hand, meaning to slap me, I think.

"That's enough." The marshal's hand came out of his pocket with the revolver still in it. He pushed the old man away from me with his other.

Mr. Spikes turned as white as his jacket. "What are you doing, sir?"

"I said that's enough. Leave him be."

Someone in the crowd behind us shouted, "He's got a gun." A lady screamed and bedlam broke loose around her.

24

Either the pistol or the woman's screaming got the knot of onlookers stirred up. That spread to the other passengers up there. Everybody went scrambling at the same time, moving away from us like they were caught in a riptide. Most of them rushed the stairs, pushing and shoving at each other to be the first one down.

The four of us plus the two crewmen stood there like fools and watched them. The marshal let his gun drop to his side, though he didn't put it in his pocket. Jimmy shook his head and smiled a little. I think he enjoyed seeing people being foolish. Made him feel smarter, I guess. The two crewmen looked at each other like they didn't know what to do. Things had just moved too far out of hand for them. They forgot about us.

The logjam on the stairs caused some panic at its tail end and a handful of people at the back turned away and headed for the wheelhouse. That's what got Mr. Spikes moving.

"Stop it. You can't go in there."

He set off for it himself, pushing people at the back aside to get to the door before the ones in front. He didn't make it. One of them grabbed the door's knob.

"Don't do that," Mr. Spikes shouted.

Before the passenger could pull open the door, though, somebody on the inside pushed out. The wheelhouse door popped open and the younger, beefy-looking crewman showed himself again. The captain must have sent him to see about the commotion.

"What's going on here?" He raised his hand like he thought that would make a difference. The crowd did pause for a second, long enough for the crewman to get a look at what was going on. His mouth gaped open when he took in the angry and fearful faces glaring at him. He looked at the people shoving each other by the stairs, and then he frowned like he was trying to figure it all out.

"He's going to kill us," somebody yelled.

"Who is?" he shouted back. Then he went up onto his toes to peer over their heads looking for us, I think. Instead of answering, the people up front started pressing together, trying to wedge their way past him into the wheelhouse. The crewman dropped down and backed up, stumbled a little, and reached for the door handle. But it had swung out of his reach. The other two crewmen had reached the door, but were pushed aside too. Mr. Spikes got knocked to his knees, but Mr. Bayles dragged him next to the cabin wall and bent over him, pushing people away to keep him from being trampled.

I couldn't see much inside the wheelhouse from where we were, but I could tell it was small with big windows that ran along the front. That crowd wouldn't fit in there. Two or three men managed to squeeze past each other and make it inside, and then a man with a body like a boulder wearing a white suit appeared at the doorway and filled the opening.

"God-damn you. Get out of here." I recognized the captain. He grabbed the next man in line, lifted him up and spun him around and pushed him back out on the deck. He went sprawling into the crowd, knocking some of them down like tenpins and opening a space near the door. Then he turned and saw the young crewman standing flat against the open door like he'd stepped back from a moving train.

"What the hell is going on?"

The crewman looked over and stood up straight. "I'm not sure, sir. There's a man with a gun..."

"Get in here and get these idiots out of here. Then lock the goddamn door. I need to get us turned around."

The crewman finally located the door handle and pulled it closed behind him. The door slammed shut and I heard it lock, which kept the rest of the passengers out except for two or three idiots inside. If the captain had to wrestle them now, I wondered who would steer the boat.

Something like a moan rose up then as people on the upper deck realized they were trapped outside. People started to scatter like ants from kerosene. Most of the ones already on the stairway had made it down by then, so the hive upstairs formed and turned around that way again.

The funny thing was that the mob had a life of its own. Nobody even looked over at us, which was where the trouble had started. The marshal had already slipped the revolver back into his coat, but it seemed like now everybody was dead set on getting off that deck even if they weren't all sure why anymore. So we just stood still and watched them. The new group of passengers crowded down the stairs until they shrunk down to a half-dozen or so. Somebody below started blowing a police whistle, probably because the panic had moved down there too.

"Let's go while we can, gentlemen," Jimmy said then. "We don't need to be here when the captain comes back out."

The marshal wasn't inclined to argue, and neither was I. We started off for the stairs. I figured we'd hide out in the passenger cabin until someone came for us.

We'd just reached the bottom when a powerful clanging noise came from up front someplace. It sounded like somebody was beating a big bell with a sledgehammer. Then the ferry pitched nose up and the deck under us dropped like a giant hand had yanked on it. I thought at first we'd hit a whale. They'd swim into the bay from time to time. The ferry started to roll to its side. I got knocked into Jimmy and both of us went sprawling. I flopped on my stomach with Jimmy right across me. I saw a line of black water roll crossways into my sight and drop away again, and the breakwater was close.

"What in damnation?"

The marshal grabbed the nearest rail with both hands and pushed his knees against it to keep from falling. His knuckles went white as foam. The boat was heaving so hard I couldn't push myself up. I heard more people screaming now, men and women both. It wasn't just a woman scared of the gun now. Jimmy rolled off me and reached for the seat of one of the benches. He pulled up onto his knees so that he looked like he was praying.

"Jesus."

"What happened?" I pulled up next to him.

The bow of the ferry yawed to port and the stern swung wide the other way. We were veering sideways, headed right for the inner breakwater. The station building near the west end was no more than a hundred yards away and closing in. We must have run onto the shallows while the captain was wrestling, and the engine kicked us into a slide. I couldn't tell if anyone was working to pull us out of it. If so, between our fast drift and the tide, we were losing headway. We weren't going to get by it. That breakwater was a mile long end to end and twenty feet wide at least. It stuck up from the water more than the height of two tall men. It was a stone wall built from thousands of boulders fitted together. If we rammed it, there was no question who'd lose out.

A wad of passengers from up in front started to crowd onto the rear deck. It was like the scene on the top deck before, only there were a lot more people this time. They fought with each other to get away from whatever was going on at the bow, and they stumbled and fell and crawled and shoved each other doing it. One man got pushed and fell down, got halfway up and stumbled again, and then almost made it to his feet. But the ship rolled and his body slapped into the rail. He flipped over it and disappeared. Somebody yelled, "Man overboard." But it didn't seem like anyone else cared. I just gaped like a dimwit at the empty place where he'd been. The ferry pitched down until it was almost level and someone up on top blew out five blasts on the ship's horn.

The marshal pushed himself off the rail and looked at me. "Get up."

I stared at his hand a second, then grabbed it, and he pulled me to my feet. He shuffled me over to the rail next to him, then let go and started sliding himself along it using both hands.

"Hold on and work your way to the back."

Jimmy stood up too and made his way toward the stern by crouching and moving hand over hand along the benches. Someone else yelled and I watched a man and woman opposite us go over the rail together. They didn't fall. They jumped on purpose, holding hands. I looked for the crewmen, but there weren't any around that I could see. Whether they were overboard or up front somewhere, I didn't know. A boy about ten grabbed one of the bumper lines and scrambled over the side, shimmying down it like a cat down a window screen. I wondered where his mom and pop went.

I worked my way down the rail toward the marshal. "We're going to hit it," I said, meaning the breakwater.

"Yep." His eyes were squeezed half closed. The skin around his eyelids was puckered up. I couldn't tell if he was as scared as I was. If he was, he didn't show it. "Get ready," he said.

I didn't know what for—jumping or crashing. Jimmy had a funny look on his face, not exactly scared, maybe nervous. He worked his way to us.

"Ready for what?"

"We get closer to that thing we'll need to jump on it."

Jimmy looked at the breakwater. "Closer? Hell, we got to jump now."

More people had jumped over and lots of them thrashed around in the water. They bobbed like corks either too scared to move or hoping someone would help them. Nobody in a white suit bothered to help that I could see. Some tried to swim to the breakwater and others had decided to try for the shore. That was a long way to swim. We were almost mile out in the bay. I saw a man get pulled under the hull and disappear like Mr. Dodson had. Somebody must have tossed a wooden lifeboat overboard. Half a dozen people crouched in it with at least twice that many swimming to it or trying to climb in. It only had one bench across the middle and shorter ones at each end. Maybe seven people could squeeze in, but not the dozen more trying to. Someone in the water grabbed for the leg of someone in the boat. A fist flew down from up there.

"Get out of there."

"Women first."

"Ball the women."

"I got kids."

"So do I."

"God-damn it."

We'd cut our distance to the breakwater by half. I could already make out words on the station house flag.

"What are we going to do, marshal?" Like I said, I wasn't much of a swimmer. He looked at me, but I could see he didn't have an answer.

"Well, you two just keep jawing," Jimmy said. "I'm going in."

He lost his jacket in the crush but managed to hold onto his beaver hat. He braced himself and took it off, held it at arm's length a bit and then sailed it over the side like a dried cow patty. "Damn. That's too bad." He squatted down then and undid his shoes.

"What are you doing?" I asked him, not very happy with his stroll in the park. Everybody else was either screaming or jumping over. He seemed to be taking his time about it all.

"Well, I ain't going in there with all my clothes on. You see those fools down there? Their clothes are going to drown them."

He pulled off his boots one at a time and tossed them over the side. Then he stood up and put his hands side by side on the rail and braced his feet against a bench. He stiffened his arms like he was going to leap over a fence.

"Get moving," he shouted. "We gotta get off this tub before it hits."

The marshal looked down at the water but didn't move.

"Let's go, marshal," I said. I wasn't keen on jumping either, but staying up there scared hell out of me.

The marshal didn't look at me.

"You can't swim, can you?" Jimmy said suddenly. He smirked as if he saw something funny in the middle of all this. He nodded as if the marshal had answered him. "I didn't think so." He turned pretty chipper for a man likely to drown. "Can't be much call for it in a cow town."

The marshal grunted. "It's not your business. You want to jump, go on."

"Guess we ain't going to Jersey then?" Jimmy said.

The marshal didn't say anything to that. The breakwater was so close now it looked big as a mountain. Slime dangled down in jagged places between the boulders. I was getting panicky myself. The marshal looked at Jimmy.

"Just go, Jimmy," he said. "Take the kid."

I looked at him and then at Jimmy. He'd stopped smiling and stared at the marshal like he was a puzzle to solve. Then he glanced at the breakwater and then at me like he was making up his mind about something.

"Aw, hell," he said. He pushed himself upright a little and half-turned toward us, keeping one hand on the rail for balance. "Okay, kid. Work your way over between me and him. I'll need your help getting him over," he said to the marshal.

The marshal nodded. With the boat rolling like it was, I sure didn't want to let go and go around him. I could see he didn't want to turn loose of the rail, but he made himself push away for me to try to squeeze under his arms, though his coat was like a curtain blocking my way.

"Hurry up, marshal. Let him get by," Jimmy said. "Here. Let go and grab my arm."

The marshal frowned and didn't do anything for a second. Jimmy was right. I couldn't get through between him and the rail. The marshal looked at me and then at Jimmy and he lifted one hand from the rail. The ferry rolled to starboard and the marshal grabbed on again. When it rolled back, he let go and grabbed Jimmy's arm. Now the marshal faced toward the bay with his hand on Jimmy's shoulder and Jimmy's back braced against the rail.

It's funny where your mind goes. I remember thinking they looked like square dancers halfway through a turn. Jimmy straightened his arm and locked his hand on the marshal's. Then the marshal let loose his other hand and took a step back from the rail so I could get by. I could see he wasn't anxious to stand that way for long.

I'd just started to slide under his open coat when Jimmy pushed off the rail and swung around behind the marshal. The marshal staggered a little anyway, so when Jimmy let go of him and shoved his back with both hands, the marshal got knocked halfway over the rail. Jimmy squatted, grabbed the bottoms of the marshal's legs and flipped him the rest of the way over. The marshal grunted, not realizing what was happening, and he didn't get a chance to ask. His head snapped back and his arms flew out and the top half of him dropped past the outside of the rail and the rest of him went after it.

Jimmy scrambled up and grabbed the rail. "He'd have stood there for all-fired forever." He was breathing hard. "You next, kid. Get moving."

I was so dumbfounded I didn't know what to do. He put a foot on the lower rail. "I got to go before he drowns. Damn fool has his boots on." He leaned into the rail and somersaulted over the side after the marshal.

25

The side of the ship by the breakwater crunched against it and sent shivers along the hull. It was loud like trees splitting, and the ferry spilled over this time. Everybody left on board went tumbling. The bow on the starboard side had slammed into the seawall. The ferry rolled to port and I thought we were going to capsize, but it righted itself a little. We stopped moving forward but the stern swung toward the breakwater like a hammer.

I looked down at the waves and all the screaming people and I knew if I didn't go now, I never would. Jimmy said I should get out of my shoes, but I was in too much of a hurry to sit down and do that. I grabbed the handrail like Jimmy had and rolled headfirst over it. I remember thinking I had got on and off the ferry the same way. It's funny where your mind goes. Next thing, I was head down underwater and trying to breathe. I came up spitting sea water and I flapped my arms around, trying to stay afloat. I should have kicked my shoes off. My legs felt like they were chained together.

Loud splintering followed a boom like thunder. The back of the ferry had smashed against the breakwater. I coughed and shook water out of my eyes and tried to pry off one of my boots. My head kept going under and I had to flail my arms to stay up, which cost me most of my breath. If I didn't get them off, I was sure to drown.

"Keep your head, kid." Jimmy floated next to me. His head stayed out of the water just fine. "Take this. Loop it under your arms and around your chest." He handed me a length of white rope and I stared at it like it was seaweed.

He reached across me and pushed it under my arm. Then he reached behind me and pulled it around to the other side and somehow tied it into a loop using one hand. I felt him tug it to check the knot.

"Okay. Lay flat on your back and spread your arms out," he said. "Hold your breath as long as you can to stay up. Don't fight. Let me do the work."

I tried to lie on my back but couldn't manage it. I saw the marshal was pulled up close to Jimmy on his other side. I couldn't tell what shape he was in, but he wasn't fighting him. He wasn't saying anything or looking around, but his eyes were open and white as hens' eggs. The flaps on his big coat floated behind him like rays. I don't know how I expected the marshal to act—maybe thrash around or curse up a fuss—but it sure wasn't like that. He just hung there in the water like a fishing cork, almost like he was waiting to die. I knew Jimmy was right about him. He didn't know how to swim.

I took a deep breath and held it, and that helped some. I followed the line of the rope with my eyes. It went from me to Jimmy, wrapped around him, and then went from him to wrap around the marshal. A lifeboat rocked in the water not far away from us. About five or six people crouched inside it. I couldn't see how many were hanging on the sides. The white rope floated like a sea snake between us and the lifeboat.

"Okay. Pull," Jimmy shouted to someone in the boat.

A man inside wrapped his end of the line around an oarlock and then another man leaned over to help him. Jimmy must have called them for help as soon as he went in. The two men tugged the rope, which swung us around backward in a line, and they started pulling Jimmy and me and the marshal toward them. My feet drifted behind me, low in the water because I never got the boots off —and the marshal probably didn't either. But at least now my head stayed up without me working at it. Jimmy held on to the rope and kicked with his own legs to help us along.

"Damn idiots," he gasped, meaning the two of us. I didn't feel like arguing.

The port hull of the ferry leaned out over us like the roof of a cave. I was afraid it would keep on rolling, but it stayed in place, hovering and rocking with a long slow motion. The other side of the ferry must have been wedged in the breakwater. It kept moving up and down, up and down, rattling and sighing like an old wooden gate and sloshing waves against my face.

Getting to that lifeboat seemed to take a lifetime. When we got near enough, Jimmy untied the marshal and helped him grab the side. He stayed that way, his body hanging straight into the water. I think he was afraid, and I don't think he liked being that or of other people knowing it. But his pride and fear of drowning nearly killed him that day.

Jimmy helped me get over next to him. Now that I had something to hold onto, I looked around and took stock. Ten or so people were hanging onto our boat. Another lifeboat floated not too far away. Sitting low in the water like I was, I couldn't see much else. I heard some splashing, which might be people swimming over to the breakwater. I wasn't as cold now as when I first went in. I was either getting used to it or getting numb.

The stern of the ferry started to swing toward us. It was bobbing faster now, like a buoy in a storm. The tide pounded on the bow, shoving it against the rocks. The space around me got lighter all of a sudden, and I looked up to see the hull rolling the other way, away from us. The motion caused another set of waves that pushed our boat and the people holding on to it farther away. The ferry kept rolling and the hull slid down the rocks, cracking and popping like fireworks. This time the roll didn't stop. The boat leaned way over to starboard and the upper deck was out of sight. The smokestack must have gone under. A plume of white steam spouted sideways into the rocks and spit its way up between the stones.

"Let's go," Jimmy shouted. "Let's go. Kick. It's going down."

He pointed further down the breakwater, yelling at us to get the boat moving. If that smokestack blew while we were this close, we'd all boil like lobsters. I leaned into the boat and started kicking as hard as I could. So did everyone else hanging on the sides. We managed to move a good way down before the boiler went. A sharp crack sounded like a house falling over, followed closely by a long hiss of steam escaping. The explosion that followed was like a hundred cannons going off at once. A black ball of coal smoke rose up from the water like it'd been belched. The decks and the passenger cabin of the ferry bulged up like a balloon. Scalding air blew across my face and I ducked under water. I came back up gagging, with flames and planks and glowing splinters and other junk falling everywhere. They showered us in a fine black snow.

I couldn't even see the lifeboat now for all the smoke in the air, but I knew it wasn't far from the breakwater. I thrashed and kicked as hard as I could to where I thought it should be. I kept going under, but then the waves or tide would push me forward. If it had been farther, I would have drowned for certain. I was spitting water when my hand smacked something hard and I groped for it and held on. We'd run into the breakwater.

The surface of the boulders was slick with moss. The waves pounded my back, knocking me into the jagged stones. But I had something solid to hang onto now, and I did. I couldn't see far, but I heard people shouting for help.

The air cleared a bit and I could see the ferry all the way over on its side, propped against the breakwater and held there. The hole in the side of it was black as missing teeth and ran the length of the hull. I took another breath and wedged my boots into the crevasse and pulled myself up so I could get a handhold on a lip of rock. I looked up the breakwater and shouted, "Help. Down here. Somebody help me."

Right away someone heard me and came over. It was one of the workers from the reporting station. He looked down and then laid himself flat and stretched his arm. I was too far below for that to work, so he got up and disappeared. I shivered and waited, figuring they'd pull the white folks out first. My shirt was torn, and I was sure I was bleeding again. Finally, a rope came snaking down from above and I grabbed it. For the second time in less than an hour, I was walking up a wall, though this one was a lot rougher. I thanked my stars I still had my shoes on. When I got to the top, I pitched forward and dropped to my knees. The man holding the other end looked to see if I was okay. I must have nodded because he went off to help someone else. I didn't get to thank him.

I managed to stand up and take a few steps along the widest part of the stones, moving away from the ferry. Half-drowned people were scattered up and down the length of it. I was cold and sore, but I was lucky to be no worse off. I was struck by how quiet it was up there. The only sounds I remember were the horseflies buzzing.

A man in dry clothes stood a few feet down the way from me, leaning over the side of the breakwater, looking down. I walked over and looked too. Our lifeboat floated right below. It was pressed against the rock wall and filled with people now, with another crowd of them hanging on the sides. I didn't see Jimmy, but the marshal had worked his way onto the lower rocks. He was picking his way up, using a dangling rope for a handhold. Darned if he wasn't still wearing that big coat. The man on top stuck out his hand, but the marshal ignored him. I guess he was too proud to take any more help.

"Get a move on, will you?" A man in the boat below him didn't look happy. He couldn't get up until the marshal got out of the way and a worried crowd clamored behind him.

The marshal looked down and gave him a scowl, and then he looked up and saw me. His face had turned a little blue, but beyond that and being soaked, he looked pretty much right. Even his eyes seemed back to normal. He didn't say anything but went back to climbing. Near the top he gave in and took the man's hand. I reached for his other arm and we helped him the last couple of feet. As soon as he was up, he let go of us and didn't say anything about it.

I looked at the bay. Whitecaps were popping up everywhere, like eyes staring at us and blinking. The chop was two to three feet and the waves broke against the breakwater like a bullwhip. Boats headed for us from all directions. Two big oar boats were on the way from the beach, stopping now and then to pick up swimmers. A trawler was wallowing over from the pier, and a small fleet of contractors' boats steamed from the outer breakwater. I could see thirty or forty people still in the water. It would take a lot of time to get to them all. The seagulls were hovering and dipping everywhere. I still couldn't find Jimmy.

The station workers had taken over the job of hauling people up. They had ropes and heavy tackle now, and it was going faster for the ones still below. I was glad to see some of the ferry crew helping too. They sure didn't seem to be much help while we were going down.

The marshal stood there looking down at the bay. His hair was strung into his face and his coat was open and his belly showed where his shirt stuck to it. I went over next to him and looked over the edge. Jimmy was right below us, treading water. He waved when he saw me.

"Hey, kid. Glad you made it."

"What are you doing down there?" I shouted.

"I ain't climbing that thing in my stockings."

"How you coming up then?" the marshal asked.

Jimmy ignored his question. "You should've learned to swim somewhere."

The marshal looked at him. "We're here, ain't we?"

"Yeah, but you're stuck out here."

"One of the boats will take us in after a bit. Get up here."

"I can swim fine," Jimmy said. His hands waved back and forth below the water. He looked like he was enjoying a dip in the pond. I wondered how he could be so at ease. It struck me that the money he stole must have been on the ferry, which meant it was gone. I wondered if he only robbed for the fun of it.

The marshal frowned at him. "Why don't you then?"

Jimmy looked around a moment and then looked up at us as if the marshal had put the idea in his head. "You know, I think I will."

"Are you crazy?" I shouted. "You know how far it is?"

"Far? Hell, that's the least of my worries. I'll probably freeze to death if I don't drown."

The marshal didn't say anything else. There wasn't much to say. Jimmy looked at me. "Take care of yourself, kid."

"What are you doing?"

He stretched out his arms and leaned back like he told me to do, sort of propping himself on them. He bent his neck up so his head was out of the water and he started to pump his legs, kicking and pushing himself backward again.

"Jimmy."

But he just moved away from us, bobbing as he went like a big slow turtle. The marshal watched until all we could see were seagulls flapping along on his trail.

"That's a long way to swim," he said quietly. I knew he was talking to himself.

If I felt better, I might have laughed. Jimmy had robbed the United States Army and the city bank, and now the one man who could make trouble for him was stuck in the bay. Jimmy was always saying luck was better than money. I wiped my face on my shirt-sleeve, not that it did much good, and looked at the marshal. His head was so low his mustache swallowed his chin.

"I guess he got away," I said.

"Not yet he ain't."

He was still set on catching him. "What do you want him for?"

"Same thing I did yesterday and the day before."

"How you going to do that, marshal? You're out here and he's swum off."

"If he makes it, he's going into town, not to the moon."

I shook my head. "If he makes it, you're still going to turn him in?"

"That's what I came here for."

"But there's no one who can say he robbed the payroll now. It's gone."

"I don't care what he did here. He has a price on him."

"He could've swum away before, but he didn't. He stayed and helped us out."

"He was trying to buy me off, hoping I'd give up on him."

"That's mean-spirited," I said. "It doesn't seem right."

I guess I sounded snotty because he looked at me.

"I ain't trying to make things seem right to you, boy."

He went back to staring at the bay. I guess the marshal didn't like being obliged to Jimmy, and he was probably too proud to admit he needed saving.

I heard a sucking sound from behind me at the end of the breakwater. Someone shouted, "She's going under."

The back end of ferry slipped down off the rocks, pulling the rest of her carcass with it. The whole thing slid into the water with a groan and went under with hardly a sound and disappeared. What was left of it were hundreds of scraps of blackened, smashed-up wood and a big smear of grease that would float up onto the beach for several weeks afterward.

26

I didn't wait for a boat back. I was soaked to the skin and getting chilled and needed to get back before I caught my death. I tried to talk the marshal into doing what Jimmy should've, which was walk to the far end the breakwater, but he didn't. I'm not sure he even heard me ask. He stared at the bay with his head tilted and his sodden coat draped over him. He didn't seem cold. In fact, he looked like one of those statues they put up after the war.

The other people on the breakwater weren't statues. They were scattered about like bodies on a real battlefield. A lot of them huddled with their knees drawn up, rocking and moaning to make the pain go away. A few of the others just walked around, shuffling back and forth but not going anywhere. Some were soaked through to the skin, and others were half-naked and bloodied up. But none seemed to notice. They had their eyes open, but it didn't look like they were seeing anything. I was half afraid one of them would step off into the bay and never even know he'd done it. Worst of all, down below me folks still in the water called for somebody to help them. But there were a lot more of them than there were boats there to pull them out. Some of those folks made the most pitiful sounds, like the whimper of whipped dogs. Even if the marshal wanted to stand there and listen, I didn't. So I walked down to the other end myself.

The east end of the breakwater extended almost to the ocean. The currents there were fast, but the cape sand curved around to a tip. I'd only be a couple hundred yards from the beach at that end. I figured that any of the small boats that came out to help would take the shorter crossing, and I knew some of the men who fished out there.

I no sooner worked my way around the east end lighthouse than I spotted a skiff putting in to the small dock. It belonged to a man named Bob who worked in a junkyard on the waterfront. I'd gone fishing with him a couple of times. He waved when he saw me, and I climbed down the rocks and got in.

Bob had the face of a hound from working so much in the sun, so when he started talking, it was hard not to stare at his face wrinkling up like old trousers. Stories of the ferry's sinking had spread pretty fast. He could see I'd been in the water, so he wanted me to tell him what happened. I didn't feel like jabbering, so I said it was all so quick I didn't see much, and he let it go.

The sea pushed back on us pretty hard, so I sat down beside him and took over one of the oars. He told me some people at the pier were the men who robbed the payroll and then they hopped the ferry right as it was pulling out. Then somebody started shooting and it made the ferry ram the breakwater. That wasn't the last cockeyed story I heard over the next few days, nor the wildest. Even the newspaper story next day was more made up than true. I could see why the marshal said he never read them.

As we rowed in, I thought about the marshal standing there watching Jimmy swim away. Sooner or later, one of the rescue boats would take him back to town. I didn't care about his business or Jimmy's, though I wondered if he'd made it back. Knowing his luck, I had no doubt he did. I wanted to get back to Miss Lil's to patch up my new cuts and get on dry clothes again. I'd changed clothes more in those couple of days than I usually did in a month. Then I wanted to find Daniel and tell him the police only knew about Tommy Dallard and also that Jimmy stole the money and then lost it. If Daniel thought the police were looking for him, there was no telling what trouble he'd get himself into.

Bob never complained once about having to take me back to shore, even though he must have thought I wasn't one needing rescue. Of course, he'd never guess I was on the ferry. He probably thought I'd got out there to fish and just jumped in to help out. He put me off near the tip of the cape and turned right back for the breakwater. He was a good man.

From where I stood, I could see most of the way down the beach. People gathered everywhere along it now. It seemed like everyone from town had come out to help. I walked back along the packed-down sand, going around the elbow of the cape and past the quarantine station. The station managers had the foreigners—or patients or prisoners, whatever they were—carrying water and blankets to the rescue boats as they came ashore.

By the time I got near the Iron Pier, I had dried off some. I figured after I cleaned up, I'd see if I could borrow Miss Lil's mare again and ride out to our cabin.

When I walked up to the house, I found her on the front porch holding a stack of blankets with both hands. She pursed her lips like I'd played hooky and pushed the blankets toward me. "Take these."

"Ma'am?"

"There was a ferry wreck, Sonny. There're a lot of people on the beach who need tending to. I'm going back inside for a tray of food."

"Um, yes, ma'am. Could I clean up first, please?"

She saw then that besides being filthy, my clothes were wet too. She couldn't have known I'd been on the ferry, so I wondered if she was worried why I looked so bad again. Maybe so, but she seemed disappointed I'd put such a thing ahead of helping out. "Just be quick about it."

"Yes, ma'am. And, uh, I need to ask you something else…"

"Don't start in now, please, while those unfortunate people are enduring so much."

"Yes, ma'am."

She nodded as if to say that was settled and turned and went inside, leaving the door open for me. I went inside and the parlor was empty. Somebody had lit a lamp. Threatening clouds had started to roll in, hurrying the daylight along its way. I put the blankets on the sofa and started for the back, when Margaret came inside with a laundry basket loaded with fresh loaves of bread.

"My Lord, Master Sonny. You look a sight again."

"Have you seen Anne?" Since I wasn't getting the mare, I decided to have it out with her instead.

I must have looked awful because instead of answering me, she said, "Oh my. You didn't have another set-to with Mr. Dodson, did you?"

She started to set the basket down, I guess so she could tend to me, but I raised my hands. "You don't need to do that. I'm fine really. Is Anne upstairs?"

I'm sure I looked wretched, but Margaret must have decided I was just filthy—not hurt—so she stopped trying to help me.

"She's at the pier helping those folks from the ferry. Did you hear?"

"Yeah. Miss Lil told me. Have you…heard anything about Jimmy?"

"He's in the back. He's in a terrible state, though. The poor man can hardly move. Came in half undressed and sopping and his teeth chattering like a drum." She shook her head like she couldn't abide all the misery that had come on to people. "He fell straight down onto the floor. Miss Lil and Anne and I had a terrible time getting him into your bed. I think he was one of them on the ferry, but he ain't said much."

Jimmy made it back and was in my bed and he was wearing my dry clothes. Miss Lil wanted me to help her out, and I needed to find Daniel. Still, with Anne at the pier, it could be a chance to square up with her. I wasn't sure where Daniel was anyway, so I decided I'd do what Miss Lil asked me. I started back to my room, but Miss Lil came into the parlor carrying a change of clothes for me.

"There it is," she said to Margaret, meaning the bread. "I've been looking all over for that."

"You were checking on Mister Jimmy, so I thought I'd take these down to the pier."

"No, no, Margaret. Let Sonny do that." Miss Lil handed me my clothes and took the basket from Margaret. "You stay here and finish the soup."

"Yes, ma'am." Margaret nodded and went back into the kitchen.

"Put those on out here and then get a move on," Miss Lil said to me. "If you go back there now, you'll bother Jimmy. He just got to sleep."

"Yes, ma'am." Sure wouldn't want to bother Jimmy.

I stood there with my clothes in my hand until she figured out I was waiting for her to leave too.

"Tell the girls we'll bring soup down in a few minutes. Ask them what else they need."

"Yes, ma'am."

She shook her head again and went to the back with Margaret.

I stripped down and used one of the blankets to towel off. The dry shirt and trousers felt like a new skin on me. I sopped water out of my shoes as best I could and put them back on. Miss Lil hadn't said whether to take the blankets or bread first. I wrapped the bread up inside one of the blankets like a hobo's sack and folded the rest of them into the basket. I could just manage to lift the whole thing. I went down the porch steps, peering around the basket to be sure I didn't miss a step. The sky was getting heavier. The wind had picked up and clouds hung overhead like wet sheets.

When I made it out to the Iron Pier, people were spread out everywhere. Many passengers who'd been brought there were wrapped in blankets. Some were lying down and others sitting hunched up, but none of them moved around very much. People scurried around giving them food and water and wrapping their cuts in bandages. I recognized a lot of those who were helping—fishermen, dock hands and even a few of the sober ones from the Clubhouse. The pier was dotted with people like tossed salt. Doctor Orr, who worked at the quarantine station, leaned over a laid-out man, holding a tube with a needle he'd stuck into the man's arm. The scene looked like battlefield hospitals I'd read about.

I found Anne with Carol at the near end of the pier. They were wearing their day clothes and both were spotted with blood. Emily and Jane might have been out there somewhere too, but the far end of the pier was so crowded I couldn't tell. Carol was wrapping cloth around the shoulder of a woman who was bleeding so fast the bandage soaked through before she could get it tied. Anne had used someone's coat to cover a man who was sprawled out and groaning. She looked up and saw me.

"Sonny, come over here and bring me those towels."

"Towels? No, this is bread and blankets." I sort of mumbled over the pile at my chin.

Anne made a face. "Okay. Put them down. Emily will come get them. We need lots more clean towels. I thought Miss Lil went back to get some."

I put the basket down. She tucked the flaps of the coat underneath the man and stood. "I'll go for them myself. Stay here and help Carol give out the bread."

Carol was standing too. The woman beside her was bleeding through her bandage. "No, Anne. You stay," she said, meaning for her to take care of the man. "I'll run on back. I can't do much more for her."

Anne nodded and squatted down again. "Let's get a blanket on him," she said to me. She slipped an arm underneath his shoulders and tried to help him sit up a little. "Come on, mister. Let's get you warm."

He looked up at her and then struggled to do it. He was trembling pretty badly. His coat was open, and his shirt was ripped down the front. His pants were sodden with muck and blood. He was an older man and must have had money from the cut of his clothes, though they were torn up now. He mumbled and closed his eyes again. His lips were blue.

"Help me get his boots and trousers off."

She started to unfasten his suspenders and I moved around to pull off his boots. Anne glanced up while she worked on him and noticed how I looked.

"What happened to you? You're a mess."

"It's been a bad day." I got one of his boots off. "Someone tried to rob the payroll and the money's gone missing." I wanted to see how much she knew, or at least what she'd tell me.

"Yes. So Miss Lil said."

She went back to popping the suspenders and started in on the buttons to his fly. The man kept mumbling, but he let her work on him without a fuss.

"Jimmy got Daniel mixed up in it. You knew he was doing it, didn't you?"

"If your brother stole that money, he made his own bed," Anne said. She didn't look at me, but she didn't act surprised by what I'd said.

"He didn't. Captain Sweetland told the mayor that Mr. Dodson still has it." I watched her face. "He said an Army captain took it to the bank a different way before the robbery."

She didn't react when I said Captain Sweetland's name. She pulled the shirttail out of the man's pants and ripped the rest of it to get it off him. He groaned. I had his other boot off, and she came around to help me pull off the trousers. His underwear was black silk. He might have been one of our guests.

"I guess Daniel got lucky then," she said.

"I'm sorry, Anne, but I know you're lying. Captain Sweetland was with you all night. He didn't even have his clothes until this morning. You had Margaret hang them out for Jimmy to use, didn't you?"

She kept looking down at what she was doing.

"I think the captain figured it out, though," I said, "after he got back to his Army boat and found out what happened. He had to blame Mr. Dodson to keep himself out of hot water."

Maybe the Army boat wasn't tied up at the pier anymore. Captain Sweetland could have used the ferry's accident as an excuse to skedaddle back to Philadelphia.

"It worked out just like Jimmy and you planned, didn't it?"

"You said your brother's all right, didn't you?" She still didn't look at me.

"No. I said he wasn't blamed for it. He thinks they're looking for him. I'm worried he'll do something crazy."

She finished drying off the man's chest and then spread out one of the blankets. She crouched by his head, lifted his shoulders and nodded at me. I raised him by his legs, and she wiggled the blanket under him with her foot. We put him back down. Then she pulled it tight and tucked it all around him.

"What do you want, Sonny?" She sat on her haunches and looked at me.

It was a good question. I guess I wanted her to tell me I had it wrong. Or at least that she was sorry.

"I want to keep him out of trouble."

"Your brother knew what he was getting into."

"I don't care about that. I just want him safe."

"Where is he now?"

"Hiding, I think."

She looked away again. "I'm sorry about your brother, but I don't know how to help."

"He saved my life once."

"I know he did. I understand why you're trying to help him now." She looked at me again. "It's the same with me and Jimmy. I don't like all he's done, but what he's done for me means more than that."

That shut me up. We sat there looking at each other, me not knowing what to say next.

"You didn't answer my question," she said then.

"What question?"

"What happened to you?"

I pointed at the man in the blanket. "The same thing that happened to him."

She frowned and then her face opened and she understood. "You were on the ferry?"

"Jimmy didn't tell you?"

She shook her head. She looked in the direction of Miss Lil's house. You could just see her roof from there. "He wasn't doing too well."

"But you knew he was on the ferry." It wasn't a question.

"I knew he was leaving." She thought about it some more and then asked, "What were you doing on there?"

"I…It's kind of complicated. I followed the marshal onboard."

"The marshal?" Her eyes opened wide round. "He went on after Jimmy? Did he make it too?"

"Make it?" I realized she felt about the marshal the way I did about Mr. Dodson. "No. I left him out there. I got a ride back."

She was getting agitated. She wasn't interested in how I was doing anymore. "Where is he now? Do you know?"

"I don't."

"He could be at the house." She stood, ready to go back there herself. I stood too.

"I just came from there. He wasn't. Besides, Miss Lil wouldn't let him in." I wanted her to stay on the pier because as soon as she left, my talking with her would be done for good. In my heart, I knew it already was.

Anne looked out to the bay end of the pier like she was deciding what to do. Doctor Orr walked toward us, slowly swinging his black leather bag. When he came up to us, he looked down at the man in the blanket.

"What's the story on this one, Anne?" The doctor tended to Miss Lil and the girls when they took ill, so he knew them all.

Anne shook her head and got back to business. "Hypothermia, I think." The doctor nodded. I wondered how she knew that word. "Should we move him to the station?"

"Anything else wrong? Is he cut or banged up, I mean?"

Anne shook her head. "Not bad that I can see. He's dazed, though. The blood looks worse than it is."

"Then he'll need to stay here. The station's beds are crowded." He knelt next to the man and felt at his neck. "You should try to get some hot liquid in him."

"Margaret's making some soup," I said. "I'll go get some."

"That would be good, Sonny," the doctor said. "Please be quick about it."

I saw from Anne's face she wanted to go too. "Check on our guest while you're there, Sonny."

"I'll be back directly," I said, but I knew I wouldn't.

27

I met Miss Lil and Margaret coming the other way. They carried a big enamel pot between them, one of them holding each handle. Margaret had a string of tin cups strung over her shoulder and tied together with a length of clothesline. They clattered like horses over stone as she walked. Miss Lil called out to me as they came near.

"My goodness, Sonny. Where have you been? Did you deliver the bread and blankets?"

"Yes, ma'am. I was helping Anne with a nearly drowned man." The soup smell coming up around the lid made my stomach growl. The only thing I had to eat that day was a biscuit. "Doctor Orr is there too, ma'am. He says he could use that soup."

She stopped walking and looked at me. Margaret stopped too and they set the pot down between them. Some of the soup splashed out when they put it down. I saw that Miss Lil was deciding whether to have me take over carrying for her. I hoped she didn't. My talk with Anne was over now, so I wanted to borrow her horse and find Daniel.

"Where are you going now?" she asked me.

"Well, ma'am, I'd like to look for my brother."

"Your brother?" She stared at me as if she'd just noticed my bedraggled state. Helping Anne with that near-drowned man got me filthy again. I looked like that so much the last few days I suppose she was getting used to it. "My land. Are you bloodied? Did he do that to you?"

"No, ma'am. It's…It's a long story. But if it's all right, I'd like to clean up a bit again and then maybe go look for him."

I saw she wanted an explanation. I didn't want to give her one, and she didn't have time for it then anyway. She shook her head a little.

"Go clean up. You can check on Jimmy while you're there. He seems to be doing better. But come back down to the pier when you get done and bring some more blankets from the girls' rooms. You can look for your brother later."

"Um…Well, I'm feeling a little lightheaded, ma'am." I said it to get out of doing more chores. But as soon as I did, I knew it was true.

"Then get something to eat," she said. She nodded at Margaret and they bent down to lift the pot.

"There's more soup on the stove, Master Sonny," Margaret said, "and some cutup chicken on the counter."

The thought of it made my mouth water.

Miss Lil wasn't letting me off, though. "Don't dally," she said. "Get done and come on down here." They picked up the pot and shuffled off down the path the way I'd come up.

I went back to the house. When I got inside, I went to the kitchen to grab a chicken leg and then I went into the back room. Jimmy was there and he was doing a lot more than better. In fact, he was standing, leaning against the wash basin, staring into the nailed-up mirror with his face soaped up and a razor in his hand. He'd been about the house. He'd taken the lamp from the parlor and set it next to him to see better. I wondered if he was shaving off his mustache. He was bare-chested and had a towel draped over his shoulders. He had on a different pair of pants now and a fresh pair of boots. He must have kept a change of clothes in Anne's room.

The bigger surprise was that the marshal was in there too, standing next to my bed. He had a chance to change his clothes too.

He must have got a ride back in right after I left. He had on trousers and a white shirt now, but no tie or hat. He wasn't wearing his coat, which was likely soaked through. His hair was damp and scraggly. His hands were pushed into his trouser pockets, but I didn't see a pistol bulging there.

"What are you doing in here?"

Jimmy looked at me in the mirror. "How ya doing, kid?"

"I told you I wouldn't let it go," the marshal said.

"How'd you know he was here?"

"Seemed likely, so I looked in the back window."

"Miss Lil will be mad when she finds out you snuck in here."

Jimmy turned around to me. "He didn't sneak in. I invited him." He gestured at the marshal with the razor and smiled as if they were old friends. "I saw him prowling around out back and thought he'd be more comfortable in here."

"Miss Lil said that was okay?"

"Miss Lil was off carrying soup. I thought she wouldn't mind."

"Well, I don't think that's so. You look pretty peppy, Jimmy. Margaret thought you were near death."

"Well, I guess I wasn't as weak as they thought."

"Or as you made out. She might not have let you come here if she knew. She's not happy with what you've been up to."

"Come on, kid. It's a miracle how dry clothes and a little rest can restore your spirits."

I guess I made a face because he went back to shaving. He trimmed the edges of his mustache but didn't cut it off.

I walked over to my bed. "Could you move?" I asked the marshal.

His mustache twitched but he moved a couple of steps away. I knelt and pulled out a dry pair of socks from underneath. I put the chicken leg down on the cot and then sat and pulled off my boots.

"I don't understand you. You're both acting like nuts from old oaks—you especially, Jimmy."

"Why? Because I'm not bad-mannered? We been through a lot out there, kid. I think we can show him some hospitality."

"No, because you let him in here knowing he wants to turn you in."

"Well, we ain't got to discussing that yet. Maybe I'll persuade him otherwise."

I shook my head, stood up and started gnawing on the chicken. It tasted better than a steak right then.

The marshal didn't seem like he was inclined to persuasion. "I ain't your guest, Ryan. I'm here for the price on you, and I mean to collect it."

Jimmy faked a frown and rubbed his chin. He was having fun with it all. "Well, that will pose a problem, won't it? It seems a shame when we were just starting to get along. Maybe we could barter, marshal."

"We're not bartering. Come on. Get your shirt on." He went to the ironing table and picked up a fresh-folded shirt. Jimmy tossed the towel aside and took it from him. He slid his arms into it and started buttoning.

"These boots are tight," he said, as if we cared about that. "Too bad I left the good ones out there." He nodded at the bay while he bent and flexed his knees a little. "What about what you owe me then?"

"For what? For pushing me overboard? You probably hoped I'd drown."

"Now don't be ugly, marshal. I could have jumped ship and swum right then, but I didn't do that, did I? Just let the two of you sort things out. You saw how I can swim." Jimmy winked at me. His eyes were wide and the marshal's were squinting. "But I came in after you, didn't I? Kept you both from getting drowned."

"That's enough blabbing. Finish up. We're going into town." The marshal's voice sounded a little further away now, though, like he was working at something.

Jimmy tucked in his shirt and buttoned his fly. "It's a ways into town, marshal. I think you'll come around to my view before we get there."

The marshal took hold of Jimmy's upper arm and led him out

to the kitchen. I could smell Jimmy's tonic all the way across the room.

"Wait, Jimmy. Do you know where Daniel might be?"

He stopped and turned around. "I don't know, kid. I told you I ain't seen him since last night." He tilted his head, nodding at the marshal. "Get him to let loose of me and maybe we can track him down for you."

I was exasperated. If he did know something about Daniel, he wasn't going to tell me. After everything, he still expected me to believe his stories. I lowered my head and went back to the chicken. The marshal prodded him, and they crossed through the kitchen and went out the rear door. Even when they got outside, I could hear Jimmy's voice through the open window.

"I just can't see this your way, marshal. What's it going to take to get it through that head of yours?"

"Get in." The traces clinked and I realized they were taking Miss Lil's wagon. She must have left it hitched up when she came rushing back to help with the ferry rescue. That put a stitch in my plans. I'd planned to take the mare without asking her. The wagon creaked as it started down the driveway.

"You know, marshal," Jimmy's voice carried clear. "I wish someone would pay you more to leave me alone than you'll get from hounding after me."

The wheels stopped rolling. "You trying to bribe me?" the marshal asked him. "If you think I'd take any of that Army money, you must think I'm a bigger fool than you are."

"Bribe? Well, that's a hell of a thing to say. I'm just saying the price put on a person's freedom seems paltry to me. Anyway, didn't you tell me the Army said their money's not missing?"

It did sound like Jimmy was offering to split that money with him, which seemed strange if he'd lost it on the ferry. After a long silence the marshal finally said, "You're a slippery snake, Jimmy, but you ain't taking a bite of me. Giddyap."

The wagon started moving again. I heard Jimmy still arguing as they went out through the gate. "Marshal, I'm just saying things aren't always what they seem. Maybe you need to know where to look."

I confess I felt a little sorry for him, being led off by the marshal. But my sorrow wasn't grievous. I was tired of wasting time with him, and I had my own problems to attend to. Anyway, Jimmy was quick-witted enough. He'd figure his way out.

I used his towel to rub the soot and blood from my face and I smoothed my hair down in the mirror. I thought about the marshal saying brothers mattered—no one else. Daniel put himself right there for me when I needed him, and now he needed me even if he didn't know it. He thought everybody had turned on him, and he could get crazy-acting when he was upset. If I didn't get to him, he might do the worst. And I wasn't sure where to look. But he was my brother and I needed to do whatever was needed.

I went back into the kitchen. The rest of the sliced-up chicken was on the countertop. Like Margaret had promised, the soup pot was steaming. I ladled some soup into a coffee cup and gulped it down like water. Miss Lil wanted me to fetch some blankets, but I had to find Daniel. I took another chicken leg and went out the front door and started down the beach to town. While I walked and ate, I thought about where to look. I decided to start by the waterfront. If Daniel was still in town, that's one place he'd try to hide.

He found a way to find me instead.

28

Daniel wasn't at the waterfront, which meant he was likely out at our cabin. The marshal had the mare, so I had to go back to Miss Lil's and wait for him to bring it back. As I came up our steps, I saw the front door was open. Maybe Miss Lil was there now. I went inside but everything was quiet. It was late in the afternoon and the curtains weren't pulled back. Even in the dim light, I could see the room was a mess. Books were pulled off the shelves, the sofa tipped over, the piano turned half around and the top open.

"Miss Lil?" Nobody answered. "Anne?"

I went into the dining room. The corner where Miss Lil worked was a mess. The desk drawers were pulled out and tossed aside and letters and bills and register books lay scattered on the floor.

"What happened here?" I said, talking to myself to take the edge off. What if Mr. Dodson had come looking for me? He thought I was one of his bank robbers. Was he trying to get his money back?

I pulled the desk out so I could look behind it. The shotgun was there. Whoever did this either missed it or didn't care about it. I wondered if it was loaded. I'd been so distracted I hadn't cleaned it in days. I knew it was empty when Anne used it to get Mr. Dodson off me. I reached for it but then something banged the floor upstairs. I went back out to the stairs and craned my neck to look up.

"Who's there?"

Something up there banged into something else and someone cursed. I knew that voice.

"Daniel?" I started up the stairs.

"Shut up," he shouted. He was slurring a little. He came to the top of the landing and stared down. His shirt hung loose and so did his tangled hair. His chest was still caked with mud from our fight. He carried a glass lamp, its smoky light bouncing on his face. I stopped on the bottom step.

"Who you talking to?" he half-shouted, as if he wanted anyone with me to hear. He bent over the rail to look.

"Nobody. What are you doing up there?"

"I heard you talking to somebody." He came down a couple of steps and stopped. "Is Jimmy there?"

"Jimmy's not here. Nobody is. Why did you do this?" Meaning the mess.

"Why do you care?"

"Because I live here, Daniel. We've got to straighten it up before Miss Lil comes back."

"Oh, her clean-up boy might get in trouble. Think the whore might whip your Indian ass?"

I stepped off the step and backed into the room a little. "I'll take care of this. You just get out of here."

His eyes flared. "I ain't leaving 'til I get what I came for."

"What're you looking for? What do you think is in here?"

"You damn well know what."

Yeah, I did. He thought Jimmy hid the payroll money in here. His free hand clenched into a fist. It wouldn't take much to provoke him.

"I don't think it's in here, Daniel. Come on. Let's get you out of here." I backed a couple steps toward the front door.

"It's here." He lifted the lamp and looked up the stairs again.

"Jimmy figured a way to steal that money. He and that whore probably hid it in her room."

I didn't think even Jimmy was that foolish, not under Miss Lil's nose, but I was never sure what he would do. When he rode off with the marshal, he was talking like it was somewhere else.

Daniel looked at me. "Now the towners are trying to stick me for it, but I'm not goin' to let 'em." He waved the lantern at me as if he'd caught me at something. "What'd they give you to turn you on me?"

"I didn't turn on you, Daniel. Jimmy used you just like he did Tommy. I tried to warn you."

"You brought that marshal to where we hid the horses. Got him chasing me while Jimmy took the money for himself."

I backed up another step. "I didn't bring him. He followed me there. He's a smart one, Daniel, but he didn't tell them about you. Jimmy's the one he wants. Nobody knows about you. They're looking for Tommy."

"Yeah well, if they find him, they come after me next." He came all the way down to the parlor with the lantern swinging beside him.

"For what? Stealing sand? The Army captain told the mayor that nothing was stolen. He said they filled those sacks to look like money and then took the payroll to the bank by a back way. Even if they catch Tommy, nothing much will happen to him."

Daniel laughed at me. "I guess the mayor told you that then. Like he'd tell you anything except 'shine my shoes.' You must think I'm ignorant."

"No. I heard them on the street talking about it."

"Hell, you even took my knife."

I forgot the marshal gave it to me. It was probably somewhere in my room. "I've got it here. I'll get it for you."

He wasn't listening anymore. He looked around the room as if deciding what else to search. Miss Lil would be back soon, I had to get him out of there.

"I'm leaving then," I said, hoping he'd come after me. I turned toward the door.

"No, you ain't."

In a single motion he set down the lamp and pulled a knife from his boot. It was shorter than the one I was keeping for him, but it looked every bit as deadly.

I stopped. "What're you doing?"

"That money's hid here someplace and you're going to show me where."

I had to find another way. I raised my hands a little and moved back into the room. "No, it's not. Jimmy still has it."

"So it's not at the bank?"

"No. Jimmy took it with him."

"Then it's here somewhere." His mood was turning dark again.

"He's gone, Daniel. He was on the ferry, the one that sank."

I saw he had no idea what I was talking about. His confused expression lasted about a second before he exploded.

"Piss on you." He brought the knife up. "You think I'll believe anything."

I backed up, knocking against the desk. "It's true. Look outside. There's bodies all over the pier."

I don't know if he thought I was lying or if his anger just boiled over onto me. He came at me with the knife and stopped when the tip was an inch from my eye.

"Stop it, Daniel.

He turned the blade sideways. It looked as big as a rail spike. His eyes went flat and cold. "You stop lying."

He swung it at my head, and I jerked my arms up. The flat caught my forearm and drew blood. "And stop running me around while he gets away." He raised both arms and came down hard on my shoulders, knocking me to my knees. I went onto my stomach and tried rolling away, but he dropped on top of me and put his knees across my chest. He pressed the heel of his knife hand on my throat.

"I should've left you at that damn school."

"Don't." I was gagging. "I'm…not…"

"Yeah you are." He straightened to look down at me. He let go of my throat and pointed the knife at my face. "You got a chance to tell me where it is, Sonny, or I'll cut your eye out."

When his weight lifted, I brought my knees together and jerked them up as hard as I could. His breath exploded like a busted pipe, and his hands flew out and he went up and over me, his knee smacking my nose. I rolled onto my stomach, knowing I had to watch him. He rolled over too and pushed up to his knees. He was breathing hard, almost panting, but he kept his eyes on me. His knife was several feet away from him near the front wall. He looked at it. I couldn't get there before he did.

"I swear to you I'm not lying. I saw Jimmy take the money on the ferry."

That was a lie, though. He watched me but didn't say anything.

The front door opened and Hannah came in. She squinted in the sudden darkness of the room. She looked down at the lamp and then at Daniel.

"My father's coming," she said. "You've got to go." She thought he was me.

"Get out of here."

"What?" She looked where my voice was. She saw me and realized her mistake. "Oh no, Sonny…"

Daniel got to his feet. "You kept me here 'til your little whore brought her daddy." He went to the wall and scooped up the knife. Hannah opened her mouth but only blinked.

"That's crazy. I didn't even know you were in here." I looked at Hannah. "I said get out of here."

Daniel pointed the knife at her. She put her hands to her face and backed away from him. "Let's see how bad he wants to get me." Two long strides and he had her hair twisted around his fist.

I scrambled for the desk, pulled it away from the wall and grabbed the shotgun. I don't know what I might have done, and I didn't find out. When I turned around again, Mr. Dodson was in the doorway. He had a gun in his hand, the one he'd fired at the ferry. And he looked as wound up as my brother.

"Daddy."

It took him a couple of seconds to figure what had happened and then he went at Daniel, whacking his face with the pistol. Daniel let go of Hannah and staggered backward, keeping his balance so he could go after her father. Hannah stumbled. Her foot kicked against the lamp and it shattered, spraying burning oil over the carpet. Dodson raised the pistol, stopping Daniel.

"I want my money," he said.

I racked the shotgun and pointed it at his stomach. I wasn't sure it was loaded. Mr. Dodson looked at me but didn't lower the pistol. Daniel looked too.

"Get out of here," I said for the third time. "Both of you." I tried to sound like I'd shoot if he didn't.

Hannah was very still. She was standing in a pool of burning oil, but she didn't look down at it. She was scared and didn't know who to be more afraid of. Mr. Dodson lowered his gun a little and moved behind her, keeping his face turned to me. She looked back and his hand snaked around her neck and he yanked her tight. He raised the pistol again. Hannah squirmed and whimpered, trying to get away. But he didn't move.

I shifted a little to one side, trying to get a clear shot, and he backed toward the door, dragging her with him.

"We ain't done, boy," Mr. Dodson said to me. He should have paid attention to my brother.

"We are," Daniel shouted and launched himself. He swung the knife backhanded, hitting Hannah in the face trying to knock her away to get to Mr. Dodson. Mr. Dodson jerked to the side but kept his feet. Daniel tripped and caught himself against the wall. Mr. Dodson pressed the gun to his daughter's head and turned to watch Daniel as he talked to me.

"Don't try anything, boy. I'll shoot her as soon as you."

Hannah twisted her head to look at me. Her eyes were pleading. I lowered the shotgun. I couldn't shoot without hitting her and Mr. Dodson's finger caressed the trigger of his gun.

Daniel was opposite me on the other side of the room and Mr. Dodson. He held the knife in front of him, edge up. "She don't matter to me," he said.

Mr. Dodson pulled the gun away from Hannah and swung it around toward Daniel. Daniel went at him, and Mr. Dodson pulled the trigger. I fired at the same time. I didn't miss.

For a second everything felt sharp, like all of us were frozen. Sparks flared in the shadows and orange flames flickered on the carpet. Nothing else moved. Then I watched the carpet melt.

Mr. Dodson twisted around like he couldn't keep his balance. His coat was ripped away and the shirt underneath was pocked everywhere with blood. He let go of Hannah and fell over. She screamed and her hands fanned the air and she went to her knees, still waving as if shooing bees away. She was coated from neck to waist in blood. Daniel stood watching Mr. Dodson as he moaned and flailed.

Hannah sprawled face down on the floor, rocking on her elbows, hands clutching at her face, mewling from the pain. Daniel looked at her and then at me, turning only his head. He frowned as if he didn't understand what happened. He looked at the shotgun, then back at my face, and smiled at me. His face was bleeding too. He turned back to stare at Mr. Dodson and shifted his knife a little. Mr. Dodson still held his gun. My shotgun was empty.

Daniel dropped on top of Mr. Dodson and pushed the blade into his face. Somehow, though, Mr. Dodson pulled the trigger, screaming like an animal while he did it. The bullet caught Daniel high on his chest. The force of it pushed him up again and his hands opened like he'd been scalded. He fell backward and didn't make a sound.

I dove for Mr. Dodson. The knife handle stuck straight out from his cheek and I couldn't see the blade. I slammed into him and yanked out the knife. He screamed, but not for long because I shoved it into his eye. He made a rattling sound like my father did that gurgled at the end.

I slid over next to Daniel. His eyes were closed. His breathing was ragged and not deep, and blood drenched him. I put my face close to his so he could hear me.

"Daniel."

He moaned.

I glanced at Hannah. She moaned, "Oh, oh, oh," and clawed at her cheeks with her fingers like she was trying to pull her face off.

I looked at Daniel.

"It's okay. I'm going for help."

He coughed. After a few breaths, he said, "Okay." His voice was raspy.

"I didn't lie to you. I love you."

His eyes stayed closed and he sucked in a breath. It didn't come back out.

"Daniel, look at me."

His eyes flickered as if he was trying to. His fingers twitched. He seemed to be reaching for my hand, but then his hand fell away. I lifted it up and pressed it to my shirt.

"Okay…broth…" he said. I could barely hear him.

I watched at his eyes, hoping to find him in there. They opened a little and he worked his lips again. Then he left and his face sagged. I pushed my cheek against his.

"Ni'mat," I said.

29

I sat in the rain with Daniel lying beside me. Even from where I was, the heat seared my skin like hot sand. Someone had found a quilt and draped it over him. It covered him all except for his face. He didn't look mad at me now or pained because I'd sold him out. His eyes were closed as if he was...not asleep, I guess. Maybe just resting. But I knew that wasn't so. He was too still, alone in a place where I couldn't reach him. I must have been out there a while because it was only drizzling and my shirt and pants were soaked through. Someone squeezed my shoulder.

"Come on, son. Let's get you out of this rain. We got to see to that nose." The marshal was there, and Anne was too, next to him. I didn't look around, and I didn't argue. I just stood. Anne didn't say anything at first. She just looked at me with sad eyes. I must have swayed because she reached for my arm to keep me from going over.

"I'm so sorry," she said then. I think she meant for Daniel, but maybe not.

"Hannah?" I said.

"Her face is bruised and she breathed in a lot of smoke, but I think she's okay. Emily brought her home."

Hannah was okay then. That should have been more important than it felt. I didn't ask about her father.

"You going to be okay?" Anne asked me. She dabbed my nose with her dress sleeve. It came away red.

My nose. Yes. My brother was dead, though. I nodded.

She shook her head a little like she realized it was a foolish question, and she looked away. Then she walked away. "I'll see if I can find you some dry clothes," she said over her shoulder. She could go do that if it made her feel better. Dry clothes didn't matter, though. She didn't hurry back.

"What happened in there?" the marshal asked.

When I didn't answer, he said, "Your brother was shot, son. Twice." As if I didn't know that. "Dodson do it? People down the beach said he was looking for you."

I looked at Daniel.

"I think he did," the marshal added. "You know where he went?"

I looked up. Where he went? I looked around me. We were on the road a little down from Miss Lil's, except the house wasn't there now. In its place, like some magician's act, an immense fire bellowed and blazed. The flames had mounted so wide and high I had to shade my eyes to look at them.

I looked at the marshal. He stared back at me and then looked at the fire. "In there?"

Again, I didn't answer him.

He shook his head a little. "That house was on fire, son, but you carried that girl out and went back in."

I didn't say anything. There wasn't anything to say.

"You brought your brother out too." He didn't say even though he was dead. He watched my face and then said, "You don't remember it, do you?"

I didn't. He squinted at me and chewed his mustache and then looked at the fire. He was thinking things over.

Miss Lil stood not far from us, watching her life burn down. She was still being herself, though. She had her arm around Margaret, who was bawling like a baby. I didn't see Jane or Carol. A couple of dozen men were closer into it, spread around on all sides. They worked in a fever, tossing buckets of bay water, trying to douse the flames. Their shirts were soaked through with sweat. A chain of men ran buckets back and forth to the beach. All of their faces had turned ham-colored and were streaked with soot. Jimmy was one of them.

Finally, the marshal said, "Won't be much to find in there once the fire burns itself out." He was still staring at it. "I think Dodson shot your brother and set fire to the house. Then he took the Army's money and hightailed it. Son of a bitch left his daughter to fend for herself. Probably won't be seeing him again." He looked at me. "Ain't that right, son?"

I understood. Nobody cared if an Indian got shot. But killing a towner—that was serious.

"You didn't turn him in," I said, meaning Jimmy.

He knew who I meant. "We ran into folks coming the other way. Word spread fast. We turned back to help."

That must have been a slow carriage ride. They left an hour before the fire started.

"Do you still mean to?" I don't know why that interested me then. I guess I needed to see how much things cost now that we'd paid for it.

The marshal looked to where Jimmy was working. "Son, you need to stop calling him Jimmy, like he's some good friend of yours. He goes by lots of nicknames, but the name he uses the most is the one on the wanted poster, Butch Cassidy, and that ain't his real name either. He's a hunted outlaw with a price on his head. But with all that's happened here, it doesn't seem to be my time to take him in."

So they'd come to an agreement. I tried to watch the fire, but my eyes kept going back to Daniel's body. "It was all wasted then."

"Not wasted, boy. You did a good thing."

"My brother doesn't think so," I said, not angrily.

He nodded. "You stood up for him. Your brother killed himself, son. Not you."

"If you and Jimmy hadn't come here, he'd be alive." I half looked at him. "So I guess you killed him too."

He looked away. It was the only time I saw him shy.

I watched the fire and tried to feel bad for Miss Lil, but it seemed far away and not very important. When the fire finally burned itself out, Miss Lil helped me wrap Daniel in the quilt. I admired her for taking any time for me then, considering what had happened to her. Emily brought the carriage back—I didn't ask after Hannah—and the marshal and I squeezed Daniel into the back of it. I wanted to put him down out at our farm, and I was ready to ride out there. But Miss Lil said we should wait until morning because it would be too dark to give him a proper burial. So we took Daniel into town instead. Miss Lil wanted to stay a bit longer to rummage through the ashes and find what she could while the light lasted. They did manage to save the stable and her barn. The little rain, miserable as it was, helped with that. But there wasn't much left of the house—just a stone chimney and a mound of charred, smoking wood taller than her head. Mr. Dodson was down in there somewhere too. But as far as I know, nobody ever figured that out.

The marshal drove the carriage and I sat backward and braced Daniel so he wouldn't fall out. The marshal stayed quiet as we rode in, but I spoke to Daniel once and said I was sorry for the way things turned out. He never believed I tried to save him. I guess because I didn't. Now there's no more I can do about it. We took Daniel to the undertaker and the marshal paid him to build a pine box for him and extra to keep him for the night. It felt peculiar leaving him there. I don't think he'd ever been in a town building before. If that undertaker thought anything of finding the bullet holes in him, nothing was ever said about it. Later on, Miss Lil came to where we were, which was at the marshal's hotel, I think, and put some ice on my nose. I don't remember much about that night. I guess I slept in one of the hotel's beds, but I couldn't tell you for certain, or even if I slept at all.

30

Next morning the marshal hired a wagon and he and I and Miss Lil —and Daniel in the box—rode out to our cabin. Miss Lil said a few things about nothing during the ride, mostly to keep my mind off Daniel. I knew she was fretting over what she'd lost, of course, but still she came along out of concern for me. She even managed to find me some clean clothes to wear, and they almost fit. I also knew she didn't like the marshal much, but she was pleasant enough to him and thanked him for helping me out. That's just the way she was.

We put Daniel in the ground next to Ma. I had the marshal help dig up our Father's grave first. By then, he was a few bones in a rotted box as useless as he was. We moved him into the woods so Ma and Daniel wouldn't have to be next to him. The marshal didn't raise a fuss about doing it, though I saw it took the wind from him. When we were all done, Miss Lil said a Christian prayer over the grave. Daniel wouldn't have liked it, but I didn't say anything because I knew she needed to do it. Before we shoveled in the dirt, I pried open the box and I looked at him. The undertaker had cleaned him up and put him in a suit of clothes, another thing he'd never worn in life. His eyes were closed, and his face was pale as a white man's. I remember thinking I could jump in with him and let them cover me too.

After we got back, the marshal took me to the Ocean House and treated me to a hot meal and a glass of whiskey. It was the first time I'd had hard liquor. We got stares for sitting in the dining room, but he didn't care and no one seemed inclined to take him on.

We didn't talk much. I didn't feel up to it and he respected that. Miss Lil was staying there too, sharing a room with Emily. Carol and Jane were local girls, so I guess they found family to stay with. Miss Lil got a room for me. The manager didn't like it, as his manner made plain, but she didn't have patience for that. She paid him twice his regular rate, so aside from more scowling, he didn't make a fuss. Anne stayed with Jimmy at the Breakwater.

In the evening, the three of us sat out on the hotel's porch, the marshal smoking his cigar like the first time I'd met him there, and Miss Lil sitting in a rocker across from us sipping wine. The night was cool, but the rain had cleared out and the stars were out. I was a little surprised Miss Lil sat with us. I guess she needed company herself. She made small talk with the marshal a while, talking about anything and everything except the fire or Daniel. I knew he didn't go in for that, but I give him credit. He made the effort. Neither of them pressed me to talk any. They were there to keep me company.

As the night wore on, Miss Lil even warmed a bit to the marshal. The wine might have helped at that. She went well past her usual one glass of sherry that night. She asked about the stories about him and he answered her politely with few words and not really telling her anything. He asked her questions too, which I figured was his way of moving the talk away from himself. By her third glass of wine, she was doing most of the talking. I found out she was born in Connecticut and that she wore black for her husband, a sea captain who drowned. Listening to them chit-chat about nothing was a comfort to me and it did take my mind off things for a little while.

The last time I saw the marshal was when he stubbed out his cigar and stood up. The porch was dark. It was well past midnight, and Miss Lil had gone up to her room a couple of hours before. I couldn't make out his face. He was a shadow in front of my chair. He said he was going to pack his bag as he was leaving first thing in the morning. The ferry company brought another boat over from Cape May. They didn't want a shipwreck to spoil the season's business. I didn't stand when the marshal did, so he stood there in the dark watching me. After a bit, he put his big hand on my shoulder and gave it a squeeze.

"Taking a life is hell," he said. "You had a hard choice to make, son." His voice got as quiet as the night.

"Do you believe in hell, marshal?"

He thought about that a minute. "I don't know. I guess hell's something preachers make up to keep folks in line."

"How about heaven?"

"I don't put much credit in an afterlife. We got to make what we can out of living. If there's a God, I reckon that's what he wants."

"Then that's all there is to it?"

He saw where I'd gone, and he gave me what he could. "Your brother could be good, I think, deep down. But he was an angry man and that twisted him around. In the end, that's the part that won out."

He didn't say more, and we both let it be.

"Marshal, can you tell me one more thing?"

"And what's that?"

"I've been calling you marshal since you came into town. Do you have a name?" If I was never going to see him again, it seemed like I should at least know who he was.

He looked at me a moment and then said, "How about Marshal Earp? Will that do?"

"Earp?" I shook my head a little, that didn't seem much of a name. "I think I'll just stick with marshal."

He smiled at that. "Good night, son. Take care of yourself."

He nodded and walked away, leaving me in the dark. I sat there a long while after. I was tired as a dog, but I didn't want that day to end. It was the last one that had Daniel in it.

I woke up in the hotel bed after the sun was long up. I had no notion of how I got there. Miss Lil must have come back down for me. I got dressed and went looking for her, but she was in town on business. I saw from the clock in the lobby that it was well past noon. The ferry had gone and the marshal with it. I didn't feel much about that at the time. But later on, I wished I'd seen him off. Later, I found out that Jimmy and Anne were gone too. They went on the same ferry as the marshal. I wondered if they'd talked on the ride over.

I missed seeing Anne off too, but I did get to say goodbye. On the day of the fire, while the marshal went to harness the mare to the carriage, Anne came back without finding any clean clothes and stood with me a while. Jimmy saw us and came over too.

"I'm sorry about your brother, kid," he said. "It's a damn shame."

It's a measure of my mood that day that I couldn't get angry at him for that. Still, there was nothing left to say back either, so we stood there feeling awkward and not knowing what else to say. Finally, Jimmy said they should be going, and he extended his hand. I took it, and he said, "Goodbye, kid." And that was that.

Anne put her hand on my shoulder and brought her face close to mine. "It wasn't your fault, Sonny. If not for you, Hannah would have died in there." I never told her about Mr. Dodson still being in there, but I think she knew. When I didn't say anything, she said. "And no matter what you think of me, please know that I care about you."

"Goodbye," is all I said. I wish I'd said more, but I didn't. She gave Miss Lil a hug and I knew she was leaving for good. I saw Miss Lil was sad, but not sad enough to talk her out of it. I watched the two of them walk down the beach. Jimmy, or I guess I should say Butch Cassidy, turned and waved once, his big moon face grinning behind that pencil mustache of his. But Anne didn't. That was the last I saw of them.

31

I read in one of the newspapers today that the marshal died. He was almost eighty years old and living out in California. His real name was Wyatt Earp, and he'd been a Deputy U.S. Marshal who'd run into trouble in a place called Tombstone, some years before he came to Lewes looking for Jimmy. According to the newspaper, he died in his sleep with his wife there beside him. If that's so, I'm glad for him, and also that he didn't have to read the newspaper's story. It churned up all the stuff about him from the old days. I don't know what's true about all that. I don't think newspapers care much. But it was peculiar wondering about him again.

I hadn't dwelt on those things for years. After a while, I wasn't upset or angry anymore, not like when it happened. Mostly, I just didn't think about it, and it's been almost thirty years now. But the news story did pull me back to those times, to that week. And those memories came back as clear as when they'd happened. I wondered if he still wore that big mustache he'd favored.

I thought after he and Jimmy and Anne left town, things might go back to being normal, at least as much as they could. It was a silly notion, of course. Daniel was dead, Hannah had gone off to live with her uncle and Miss Lil's place was burned to the ground.

For a while, Miss Lil made a fuss to people over how I'd rushed into the house while it was on fire and brought Hannah out safe. But with Mr. Dodson and the money gone missing, someone had to take the blame. Word got around that Mr. Dodson had run off with a whore. Tommy Dallard vanished like smoke. I heard he joined the Army over in Baltimore. With Daniel dead, it worked out for everybody if he was the one. After all, everyone knew he was a no-account Indian. One of the city policemen told folks Daniel had gone to Miss Lil's to hide the money and that it burned up in the fire he set. Then someone else decided I was the one who let him in, and that was the story that took hold. It had to be the truth, because it got written up that way in the *Pilot*. In the end, it didn't matter what was true because it wasn't long before interest in the robbery and the fire and even in Mr. Dodson—"how sad for his daughter"—died out, and other gossip took its place.

The Army and the bank argued over the money a while. But when all was said and done, they divided the loss between them. Jimmy's name never got mentioned. I didn't stay in Lewes long after that. When I told Miss Lil I was going, she didn't argue. She didn't have a place for me anyway. She bought me a ferry ticket, though, and loaned me some money, all of which I paid back in time.

I saw Hannah once before I left. I was on Second Street with Miss Lil and as we went by the bank, Hannah was coming out of it. She was with a wrinkled and sour man. I found out later he was her uncle. She looked up and saw me and I started to smile. I lifted my hand and put it down again. She stood where she was, following me with her eyes as our carriage went past. She was pretty as ever and I could almost smell her perfume. But she seemed younger to me somehow. She didn't wave and she didn't smile, and the look she gave me was odd. Not friendly but not hateful either—mostly just sad. I looked away. I used Miss Lil's ferry ticket the next day.

I don't know where Anne went or how long she stayed with Jimmy. But I am sure he landed on his feet. I think the only one he cared for was himself. By some estimates, more than twenty thousand dollars went missing from that robbery. If he had it, I hope he and she lived high on it, because Daniel never got to.

The marshal was a different sort. From what he told me, he spent his life running away from the lies people told about him. I know how he felt. That last night on the hotel porch, I asked him where he thought the money was.

"Can't say," he said. I didn't know if he meant he didn't know or just wouldn't say.

"I heard Jimmy tell you that he'd give you some of it."

He puffed on his cigar before he answered me. "It don't matter where it is, son. Having it won't make things right."

I thought he was talking about Daniel. Since then, I'm not sure. I wonder if it bought him any peace, and now he's dead too. I guess Daniel's dying didn't buy much for anyone in the end. He saved me once, but I never could save him. Remembering him is all I can do for him now.

ACKNOWLEDGMENTS

Though *The Outliers* is a work of historical fiction, some of what happens might be true. For example, Lillie Lawrence, known as Miss Lil, was a real person. She operated two small brothels in homes she owned on Lewes Beach during the early part of the 20th century, and whose occupants listed their occupations as "housekeeper." In 1900 Miss Lil's house was located at the near end of the Iron Pier, which was built by the U.S. Government in the late 1800s.

My thanks to Hazel Brittingham of the Lewes Historical Society, and a rcspcctcd local historian, for providing me with the true story of Miss Lil. There is a chapter written by Hazel that's devoted to Lil in Volume III of the Journal of the Lewes Historical Society.

My thanks also to Susan Sutphin, editor and author at Cat & Mouse Press, whose review and revision of an earlier version of *The Outliers* made it a much improved manuscript.

And last, but certainly not least, my deepest thanks to Ron Sauder, my editor and publisher at Secant Publishing, for the time and energy he put in to help me revise and improve my book even further. If you find the *The Outliers* terrific reading, it's because of Ron.

ABOUT THE AUTHOR

Jack Clemons is both an author and a "rocket scientist." He has a master's degree in aerospace engineering and was an engineer and team leader on NASA's Apollo and Space Shuttle programs. Jack has authored several works of historical fiction and science fiction and he's an active member of the Science Fiction and Fantasy Writers of America. In 2018 he was awarded an Established Artist Fellowship Grant for Literary Fiction by the Delaware Division of the Arts for his short stories based on *The Outliers*. His award-winning book *Safely to Earth: The Men and Women Who Brought the Astronauts Home*, a memoir of his time on NASA's Apollo and Space Shuttle programs, was published by University Press of Florida in 2018.

www.ingramcontent.com/pod-product-compliance
Lightning Source LLC
Chambersburg PA
CBHW030544310726
48979CB00010B/2026/J

* 9 7 8 1 9 4 4 9 6 2 9 1 3 *